IMPERVIOUS

THE ASCENSION SERIES
BOOK ONE

Heather Letto

Copyright © 2014 by Heather Letto
Editor: Whitney Evans, Sun's Golden Ray Publishing
Cover Design: Anita B. Carroll @race-point.com
ISBN-13: 978-1507860076
ISBN-10: 1507860072

"If anyone has ears to hear, let them hear."

Mark 4:23

Chapter One

A late night at the unsanctioned gaming hubs equaled an early-morning skull-crusher. Because the holographic acquaintances known as Graphies had kept Fran entertained well into the wee hours, her parboiled brain now begged for more shut eye. However, hunger trumped headache.

Always.

With a yawn followed by a raspy wince, Fran rolled onto her side, lifted onto all fours, and began her morning crawl through the familiar maze of the ventilation system. As she turned her head, the ends of her dreadlocks scraped canvas clad shoulders and she smiled into the darkness. The grime spoke of who she was.

A Rebel.

Sure, she had choices. One—live within the guidelines of an Accountable resident and permit Superior eyes to monitor her every move like a true sellout, or Two—exist off the grid. Accountable to no one.

Fran considered the monthly check-ins and sharing of residential stats. *Who are you? What is your parentage and classification? Where do you live? Daily agenda? How many credits remaining?*

Nope. The Impervious authorities did not need to be in her business. Then again, as far as the Council was concerned, an Unaccountable Rebel didn't need a daily allowance.

Like food. Or shelter.

Whatever. Just a mindless system for mindless sellouts anyway. Fran moved through gritty shadows remembering what her old mentor, Chan, had shared back when he first took her under his wing.

"You just don't run with the pack, do you, Fran? Careful, life can be tricky for a lone wolf."

She snickered as the image of a mangy, rabid canine gnawing on the leftovers of a dead carcass flashed in her mind. *I'm on the prowl. Dinner will soon be served.*

Safe from the prying eyes of security, hidden in her own dark world, she trekked toward the Agora—the nucleus of the underground city of Impervious. She approached a T-junction with caution and pounded the side of the vent to announce her arrival. Didn't want to careen into a fellow Rebel moving in from the other direction. The ensuing silence indicated *all clear*, and she rounded the turn. At the next juncture, she peeked left and noticed Folsom's niche illuminated in a murky yellow light. A clinking sound told her he was hard at work creating gadgets. Although he opted not to discuss his pre-Rebel life, rumors heralded Folsom to have been a wizard of an inventor. He certainly had the look of a crazy scientist with his untamed hair and weird, shifty eyes. Fran sometimes wondered what happened in his life to send him off the grid.

She whooped down his shaft to send a greeting and kept moving. Before long, she saw the familiar glow from the tunnel's end. Just the same, she could have closed her eyes and followed her nose the rest of the way. During the dynamic hours, while the residents fed their impulsive lifestyles and incessant cravings, the spicy smell of society spilled out from the heart of the city and wafted through the vents. And since every resident hurried through the hub at least once during their hectic day armed with a hungry appetite, Fran deemed the Agora a perfect hunting ground.

She chose an exit—her favorite—cloaked behind a line of potted palms. Thanks to her Rebel training under Chan's expert tutelage, she knew just where the Council hid the sensor panel. Amongst other things, her mentor was an HVAC pro. Therefore, he knew everything from schematics and layout of this convoluted air system to the magic of shutting out the prying eyes of security.

She waved a hand over a beam emitting from a corner of the vent, and the sliver of light morphed into a holographic 3D keypad. After swiping in the code and remembering to execute the covert override keys, she sighed and waited for the screen to hum open.

Her thoughts turned again to Chan. She missed him. But like so many others, he had succumbed to the Beast through the dreaded decline a few weeks prior. Even worse, he'd rejected Rebel status and reemerged — *Accountable* – for treatment. Fran still wrestled with the concept of Chan departing from the Rebel pack. On one hand, he did need the care as he declined. On the other hand, his whereabouts haunted her. At least Chan had passed on superior training of the tunnel systems before he'd gone under.

The rigid mesh slid to the right and disappeared into the wall. Fran slithered out, stretched her cramped back, and merged into the stream of residents. While wiping dirty fingers onto her canvas pants, she assumed the swagger of a mid-lifer — proud to have outgrown the juvie years and not yet having to consider the awful decline. In this little universe, fifteen was golden. Although the stodgy Council had no appetite for all the glitter and sparkle, music and games, of mid-lifers, they knew how to purchase the hearts of this generation.

Her generation.

Gen Four.

Fran couldn't decide if she admired or despised their slick shenanigans. Maybe a little of both.

She passed a trio of holographic mimes begging for attention as she moved toward the center of the hub. Pixilated billboards rose every few feet, and clusters of mid-lifers hovered around their preferred gaming board cheering on crowd-pleasing avatars. Fran peeked over the heads of the gamers at the *band de jour* as it rocked synthetic tunes on a three-dimensional video screen suspended dead center over the Agora. The mammoth video could be seen from just about any location in the hub, and below it a herculean center stage boasted live dancers moving through a well-choreographed routine.

The Council's pièce de résistance towered in the background. Shimmering with six stories of upscale retailers, executive offices, and cybernetic vacation pods, the free-standing high-rise dwarfed the residents with affluent magnitude. Probably fashioned to keep Accountable eyes facing the sliver dome, Fran figured, as she scanned the crowd on the lookout for food.

Residents treasured food credits, yet spent them like ravenous gluttons. Because of that, her conscience remained unfettered while snatching crumbs from their super-sized appetite. She hoped for an unwatched nibbler packet or discarded meal carton — even better if still warm. Maybe today she'd get lucky and snag a fresh, unopened tin. Her own greedy taste buds danced in anticipation.

Graphies — holographs tasked with everything from advertising and food service to security detail — wandered the periphery as shoulders bumped and elbows jabbed in the congested flow of humanity. Their invisible power currents itched Fran's skin, and she scraped at her arms to ward off their insult. Most folks didn't think twice about the pixilated presence, but because of the roaming holographic city patrols, Fran always did. With these security Graphies, the Council monitored every heart that beat out of time and noticed every locked door that opened. To stay a step ahead, successful Rebels perfected the art of invisibility — speed and camouflage.

She could practically hear Chan's warning. *"Get out and blend in, Wolf."*

Which she always did.

Sometimes, however, the idea of 3-D image patrols doing the work of real men sent a wave of frustration through her gut. In reality, a geek squad ran the whole show from a well-protected office like a bunch of cowards. While munching on salty snacks, they could swipe an icon and bag a lawbreaker before brushing the crumbs from their bloated fingers. Then again, the last time she gazed into the very lifelike sockets of a patrol had been mere moments before a high voltage electromagnetic pulse shot through her body. Fran cringed with the memory.

While she roamed, she scanned the faces in the crowd, half hoping she might see a familiar set of brown eyes. Would he be sipping an espresso at a café table? Laughing it up with his new bride? Although Accountable residents considered Rebels to be traitors and deserters, from Fran's point of view, her Accountable brother had thrown in the towel long before she'd gone off the grid. And right after the invisible Beast stole their mother, no less. *Cold, Ted. Definitely, cold.*

The hurt was like an old wound with a crusty scab—never healing because of the perpetual picking. She remembered the look of confusion and pain on her mother's face the day before they brought Mom to the Ranch. Fran's eyes watered. *Nope. Don't go there.* Chan taught her not to dwell on the season of life that sent her to the land of the Unaccountable. He saw how mad she got. "*Keep your focus on today,*" he would say.

Even still...

How long had it been since she'd seen Ted? Were he and Nissa nearing their first anniversary already? Fran's jaw tightened, and the muscles in her neck seized up. She assumed her brother would have been jarred with a little wake-up call to find his baby sister missing upon return from his cyber-moon escape. *Wrong.* Fran drew in a breath and held it tight in her lungs. And to add insult to injury, when Fran temporarily gave up on the air vents and returned home after a harrowing first month as a Rebel, she'd been met with a vacated residence. Ted and Nissa? Nowhere to be found.

Hot breath hissed through clamped teeth, and her hands balled into tight fists. *Chan was right. Enough reminiscing. Time to chow down.*

As she neared the food hub, Fran spied a trio of mid-life femmes flaunting mock-maturity at the Bistro. The rookie-wives heralded their novel marital status with a wave of slim hands—the wedding tattoos so fresh Fran could have sworn she smelled wet ink. Unopened meals sat ignored on the small café table, and a nearby Graphie made a game of miming their actions.

Although nauseated by the hollow laughter, Fran sashayed a little closer. The allure of fresh, oily chips hung thick in the air, and primal urges moved her forward with the hopes of finding a burger hidden in the aluminum packet.

She felt the squeeze of her stomach, followed by another lengthy rumble. Her mouth watered. With a well-trained hand, she snatched the bounty and slipped the packet into her front pouch. Then, like a Graphie, she evaporated back into the crowd before she heard the shriek.

"Rebel! A Rebel snatched my food portion!"
Game on! Eyes to the ground and move.

Hot adrenaline shot through Fran's veins, and she jumped into the synchronous human river which encircled the hub. Human camouflage was good. However, while concealed within the throng of humanity, the flow moved her farther away from her exit venting.

An itchy electromagnescence heralded a nearby Graphie. A small panic rose in Fran's chest. To get back to the flue for escape, she would need to circle the entire Agora with this stream of residents. Judging from the rise of the fine hairs on her arms, she didn't have time for that. She needed a new exit—pronto. Her gaze flicked right and left on the hunt for an alternative outlet. She spied one about two-hundred paces out.

A hum in her ears came a moment prior to a full-body buzz announcing the arrival of the holograph.

Stay calm. Eyes down.

Anxious strides propelled her forward, and she unleashed an elbow into the soft middle of a slow-walker. As the air heaved from his lungs, he stepped aside with a grimace and an eye roll. Fran felt another current ripple down her spine. She stared at her second-hand boots and held her breath. Soon a set of rugged footwear, similar to the ones she wore, glimmered beside her own. Her gaze meandered up the thin legs of the Graphie, and she came face-to-face with a walking billboard for sporty apparel. Far-too-white, pixelated teeth flashed Fran a counterfeit smile.

"I just love my new walking-fit mesh pants. You should try a pair. They're on sale at Fresno's until sixteen hundred!"

Fran's eyes dipped back to her feet, hopeful a patrol hadn't nailed her while the Graphie advertiser had pitched the sale. She flicked a look toward a nearby vent which she now guessed to be about thirty paces out.

Suddenly, an intense jolt rippled through her core, and as if an invisible net had been dropped, she — as well as the surrounding residents — became locked in a weighty electromagnetic field. A shimmery translucence began to buzz and pop. A head taller than the tallest resident, a security guard pixilated to life. His form rippled as waves of energy rolled from head to toe. As if drawn to his presence, each resident lifted their face for a quick flash of a laser and automatically linked to the system.

Fran kept her eyes down, hoping to buy herself a few extra moments. Experience had taught her the initial paralysis only had a ten second hold before a quick release. Maybe the geek upstairs in HQ could only hold the icon steady for ten second intervals, or maybe that was just the way the system worked. Whatever. What she did know for sure was that the microcosm of release would mark her exit.

She counted down the seconds and sized up her path, envisioning the foot placement of her boots and every obstacle that might hinder a swift exit. As she felt the gradual dissipation of the paralysis, she clenched and released her fists, waking her hands from their momentary incapacitation. Life tingled back into her legs, and she wiggled her toes and hips getting ready for the sprint.

Thirty paces? Not a problem. Fran swallowed an extra-large gulp of air.

Go!

She owned the next twelve seconds. If timing proved accurate, by the time the ghostly guards reached scanning range, she would be back in the belly of the underground city, hidden from the eyes of the Council.

In spite of her heavy boots, she reached her exit in less than eight seconds. She brushed the beam, entered the code, and drummed her fingers on the stiff screen. Her heart thumped twice for each second that passed as she ticked off the time in her head.

Nine. Ten...

The hairs on the back of her neck rose. A hum preceded the body buzz.

Come on.

Eleven.

A popping and crackling sound danced at the edges of her brain, and a semi-pixilated human figure ordered Fran to halt.

Twelve!

Chapter Two

Fran dove through the opening and scurried off on hands and knees like a rat through a maze. The Graphie's field must have nipped her toes and her feet tingled as she crawled.

Too close.

On an exhale, she shook her ratty dreads.

Sixty paces to the 'T' and take a left.

Fran moved to the beat of the loud pulsations in her head as the muffled chaos from the Agora faded, and her heart settled. With her mind still in the Agora, she rounded the 'T' and ran headlong into another Rebel. The air woofed from her lungs as their bodies collided.

"Who's there?"

"Derrick. You?"

"Wolf."

Most Rebels knew the Wolf. She'd been Chan's right hand man for the past six months earning her due respect.

"Sorry, Wolf. I'll try to be more careful."

"No worries, Derrick. But, hey, the Agora's hot right now. Remember — Get out and blend in."

"Thanks, for the heads up, Wolf."

After a clumsy shift of positions, Fran continued moving away from the Agora and Derrick thumped his way to the hub. While she crawled through the vent, she whispered the sequence of strides, and the map embedded in her head came to life. The complex configuration wasn't a place for the fainthearted, and if not careful, a Rebel could get turned around and slink through this maze to her death.

She continued creeping through the network of pipes with a cool seventy-two-degree draft at her back until she came to her usual resting place where she kept her canvas blanket and a Light-Genie.

With a wave of her hand, the Genie came to life and while illuminated in its pale light, Fran pulled out the food pack and peeled back the aluminum. She inhaled the heady aroma, and the corners of her mouth lifted in a smile. No burger, but it looked like a double order of fries lay in her near future.

Fran snatched a fistful of the greasy gems and proceeded to chomp and slurp her way to the bottom of the tin. After licking the last granule of salt from her fingers, she leaned back into the metal wall and let out a hearty belch. With her belly now satiated, she allowed her head to rest. Ketchup encrusted the corners of her mouth, and Fran's eyes drooped with sleep. Soon, the Genie faded to dark.

.~.

What seemed like only a few minutes later, Fran bolted awake and, on instinct, smacked at the hand touching her arm.

"Whoa, Wolf." Pete recoiled.

He smelled like dirty hair and yesterday's cologne sample, which somehow soothed Fran's racing heart. She smiled a secret smile, almost sorry she'd slapped his hand away.

"What's the matter with you, Pete? You've been a Rebel long enough to know, 'Sleep light, wired tight.' For crying out loud, we're survivalists!"

"Yeah, sorry, Fran… Lost my head."

Although glad Pete had aligned himself with the Rebels, Fran wondered if he understood the arrangement. After all, with him now Unaccountable, Pete's greedy big sis had full claim to the family coin. She shrugged and powered up the Light Genie. Pete's stupid grin greeted her from the shadows.

"What do you want?" Her nerves bristled — partly because of the interrupted sleep and partly because of Pete's moronic expression. He clasped his hands and their silhouette resembled a gaping mouth on the overhead pipe. He moved the shadow to the edge of shadowy frizz that rose from Fran's head while making chomping and growling sounds.

"Pete!" She glared hoping to look intimidating. Maybe even ruthless.

Pete's eyes remained lit with amusement. "You don't know what day it is, do you?" He laced his fingers behind his head and leaned back into the pipe before giving Fran a sideways glance and adding, "It's Procession Day."

Fran bit her lip. "Seriously? Today's the fifth?"

"Yep."

She sighed and dropped the canvas coverlet from her shoulders unsure of the moment she'd begun to lose track of time. Then again, she didn't care much either.

"Let's go."

She crawled over the empty aluminum carton and began the trek toward the Agora. The Light Genie faded as Pete skittered behind her. Together they followed the twists and turns of the dark labyrinth like blind rodents with heightened tactile senses. Every now and then Pete would "whoop," alerting Fran that they'd passed another Rebel's hideout. Fran preferred to save her whoops for the few that mattered most in her world and focused, instead, on the venting schematics in her head.

Because she'd never watched a Forfeiture Procession in person, nervous anticipation mounted in Fran's gut. As a child, Mom had restricted Fran from such things, and by the time she'd achieved legal viewing age, she had already assumed Rebel status. Yet, for whatever reason, when together, she and Pete couldn't help but snoop. Anyway, as much as she hated it, she needed to see for herself what the Council had fashioned …which spurred another idea.

"Hey, Pete, let's get a look at the Viewing Loft first." Fran had no intention of watching the procession from up there, but figured Pete would get a kick out of seeing the big dogs in their natural habitat. Pete agreed, and they scurried off through the long shaft that ran across the sky-high ceiling of the Agora—their personal bridge from the East to the West Courts. The suspended tunnel swayed as they scampered, and Fran smiled into the darkness as Pete's breathing picked up. When they exited the bridge, Fran took a hard left and moved to the shaft that sat over the Viewing Loft where the Superiors would be seated.

Pete bellied up next to her, and their bodies mushed together in the close quarters. She started to nudge Pete in the ribs but decided she didn't mind the warmth emanating from his skin. After all, the air felt a little frosty on this side of the Agora.

"Look. The Seven are being seated."

Pete sounded like a kid who had just spotted his favorite gamer, and Fran craned her neck to get a better view through the mesh screen. The Elite Seven — the highest of all the Superiors — were ushered in first. Garbed in black from shoulders to shoes, the Seven were escorted to a row of ornate, wooden and velvet thrones. The remaining Superiors filed in behind wearing fancy red suit jackets and charcoal pleated slacks, and took their seats toward the rear of the loft.

The throne of Marcus sat elevated just a hint above the others. From her perch, Fran had a perfect view of the sagging flaps of skin surrounding his neck and jowls. His nose stood out like a mottled trumpet from the center of a skeletal expression. This monstrosity of a face often resided upon the aged. Thankfully, she'd probably never experience that season of life. It looked hideous. Like death.

Her gaze flicked over the rest of the dais. To Marcus' left sat his four revered cronies and to his right, the Sons of the Generations — Marcus, his son, and grandson.

Ethan, the prized grandbaby, sat to his own father's right hand and wore a smug look of superiority on his pale-white face.

"Is he an albino?" Pete whispered.

Fran shook her head 'no' as she focused on Ethan's demon-black eyes. A tingle of fear danced in her belly. She noticed Marcus lean over his indifferent-appearing offspring to chat with Ethan. They shared in a hearty guffaw and Ethan elbowed his father, whose skin sagged from too many years of wear. His chin wedged onto a concave chest, and thick lids drooped over unseeing eyes. After getting no response, Ethan rolled his eyes and nudged Marcus who responded with a shake of his balding head.

She'd seen enough. Fran turned to Pete, and pointed behind them. Pete understood, and the two caterpillared backwards. She encouraged Pete to take the lead as they crawled along the switchbacks bringing them back down to floor level, but when they came upon a large vent opening, she yanked on his foot.

"This spot looks good."

Besides the mesh of the screen and a few empty café tables, no obstructions stood between them and the stage. Pete mashed his face onto the solid weave, which—because she knew he would end up with the imprint on his face—gave Fran wicked pleasure. She wasn't sure if he tried to look stupid or if it was innate. Either way, "mesh face" brought a small slice of delight into her life.

They sat in silence as the moments ticked by, bringing the Procession closer. Fran's stomach knotted. *One of these days, I'm going to know someone in that lineup. Then what?*

Impervious residents had tagged the event, *The Procession of the Esteemed Ones*. Yet as far as Fran was concerned, this pageant celebrated nothing. *Esteemed Forfeiture? Hardly. More like murder. Plain and simple.*

The entire West Court had been cleared, forcing a few thousand folks to either head back to their resident pods or remain corralled in the smaller East Court to await the pageant. The billboards displayed simple white screens, and not one Graphie lurked in the crowd. After all, Impervious etiquette deemed advertising and gaming uncouth—irreverent even—during such a hallowed event. Fran snorted at the irony.

As the spectacle began, loud music filled the Agora and bounced off the surrounding structures. Although Fran assumed the song to be celebratory, from where she sat, the cacophony of music felt like an insult to her senses.

"There they are!" Pete's whisper came out on a hiss, and he pointed to the edge of the court.

A line of a dozen forfeitures, each garbed in a velvety robe, moved forward onto the main stage. Fran felt a small choke in her throat. They looked so regal, so noble, with heads lifted high and each set of eyes staring straight ahead. These twelve, each a celebrity in their own right, had been the talk of the city for the past six months.

Crafted by the Council to personal perfection, they'd lived as superstars, achieving the type of fame everyone secretly desired, loved, and envied with equal fervor. Six months of celeb-status only told of half of the story, though. Forfeitures also garnered the Superior's antidote during that time to assure they stayed at their peak. An untimely decline could render the whole charade a failure.

Today, they took their final walk as heroes. Ones who, with the help of the Council, had beat the Beast at his own game.

"Hey, look… third in line, Wolf. It's Gillius!" Pete shouldered Fran with the excitement of a child and burst into a fit of laughter. Fran responded with a sharp elbow into his ribs, and he swore under his breath before softening his voice.

"Remember when the Council unveiled him as *Corpus Perfectos*?" Pete snickered. "Hardly perfect, I'd say. He couldn't even straighten his ripped guns with all that meat in the way. And did you know that his massive legs developed callouses from the rubbing? I personally renamed him Gillius Thunder thighs."

Pete continued with muffled laughter, and although Gillius did look bizarre, Fran didn't share his amusement. Instead, she felt a pang in her stomach as she remembered his unveiling half a year ago when she and Chan had watched the spectacle on his pirated reader. In her mind's eye, she saw Chan's dark ponytail whipping from side-to-side as he tossed his head back with laughter. His eyes had all but disappeared into his face, only to be marked by tears as they streamed over the hollows of his cheek and dammed up at his strappy beard.

Unlike Chan and her, however, Impervious residents reveled in the Council's theatrics. So much so, most Gen-Threes, and even a handful of Gen-Fours, clamored for a shot at the gold. The girls at school had gushed about how cool it would be to become a forfeiture one day and bemoaned the new waiting list.

Each forfeiture received a stage name: Gillius the Great (aka Thunder thighs), Roberto the Rock, Cheyenne the Shy One, and so on. Today, however, they would each be revered by their birth name.

Fran spied Gillius, third in line, in front of a girl with a sleek chestnut mane. Like the others, Gillius' left fist rested on his chest, pinky pointed upward as he gave honor to the great city of Impervious. His glassy stare screamed of the venom already snaking through his veins, soon to bring an end to his life.

A shudder shook Fran as she wondered about corporeal termination. Rumors spoke of an excruciating end where the forfeitures dropped into agonizing spasms of death during the final pageant. Fran shivered again and reminded herself that sensationalism stemmed from useless gossip which, in turn, always led to melodrama. Then again, the entire event was absurd, so why not?

She questioned whether she and Pete should even be there, gawking like a typical resident as the parade worked their way down the stairs from center stage to the outside rim of the circle. They began an official promenade moving as one unit, soundlessly, like a snake slithers through tall grasses. Right behind Gillius, the girl—*what's her name?*—moved with the grace of a dancer, while glowing hair cascaded about her shoulders like the velvety train of her robe.

Chestnut Peak—that was it.

As the procession moved closer, Fran could make out their facial features with better clarity. Chestnut's obvious youth surprised her. As far as she knew, no one under twenty-five had ever forfeited, yet this girl still had the look of a mid-lifer, like Fran.

The line swayed with rhythmic motion, and soon snaked only fifteen feet or so away from the venting where Fran and Pete hid. The eerie silence enshrouding the promenade morphed into the sound of rushing air. A dozen pairs of slippers moved in a whisper just a few inches from Fran's eyes. When the fourth set of feet swished into her line of vision, Fran noticed a hesitation.

"Ladies and gentlemen, would you please bow your heads as Sasha Lee Dees surrenders, and we give honor to her name."

Sasha? Fran sucked in her breath.

The entire march halted. A deafening silence reverberated through the courts followed by horrific gurgling sounds. Then, Sasha dropped to the floor. Not more than a few feet from where Fran sat tucked into the venting, her chestnut head rolled from side to side and her eyes shone like polished black orbs.

Back when Fran still lived in the Old East Wing, Sasha had visited their pod once or twice to work with Ted on his macros. Fran remembered spying on them from her doorway, hoping to catch her brother making a move or something. She could almost hear Sasha's easy laughter and witty remarks.

Now, however, her eyes locked onto Fran's as if screaming for help. Her face contorted, and her body trembled. Fran felt a vibration move through her own body as her nerves quivered in sympathetic pain. Sasha's arms and legs splayed and spasmed as her back arched and head thrashed about. A sickening, acrid odor, like a mix of poison and death, wafted from the velvety robe, and bile rose in Fran's throat. Finally, Sasha's eyes rolled back into her head, and her movement terminated.

A cheer erupted from the crowd who loitered on overhead balconies and platforms, and Fran clasped her hands over her mouth to stifle the scream that roared through her body. All Accountable residents of legal viewing age watched the event. It was a big deal. Although some probably scrutinized from a small screen in the comfort of their living pods, too many just couldn't resist the sick urge to watch it live.

The cheers finally died down, and when reverence returned, the swishing slippers resumed. The seven forfeitures in line behind Sasha tiptoed over the fallen body and continued the march, leaving Sasha where she dropped. Fran could see this pilgrimage would continue until all twelve fell. She also knew she couldn't stomach another fall.

After throwing a quick elbow into Pete's side, she inched backwards until the opening became wide enough to turn around completely. She moved through the darkness with a million questions haunting her mind.

Why choose to end your life before even turning twenty, Sasha?

Fran already knew the answer… and hated it. Anyone not born to be a Superior had two choices. One: lose your mind and evaporate into oblivion, or two: trade your life for a half-year of fame and fortune as well as a smidgeon of the highly-coveted antidote.

Anger burned Fran's cheeks. The Epoch—the notion that one day they all might be freed from this city and its accompanying illness—remained the single hope that kept her alive, no matter how far-fetched it sounded. And for all it was worth, Sasha could have missed it by one day.

Chapter Three

Fran sprawled in her metal alcove and chewed the ragged skin around her nails. Since the procession yesterday, she'd spent ample time ruminating on the condition of her old mentor while spitting dead skin onto the low ceiling overhead. She hadn't checked on him in a few days, so she ought to pay him a visit.

Fran shivered, but not from the prospect of seeing Chan. Rather, at the thought of revisiting the Beast—the invisible face of death which pervaded every hallway of the Ranch. Its malevolence pricked at her skin and left a stench in her nose. She spit one more hangnail onto the ceiling before rolling onto her side and, on a groan, moved away from her comfy niche.

Visiting Chan felt serious. Solemn. Reverential with no leeway for malarkey. Therefore, she opted not to invite Pete to this one. Not to mention the fact she knew she was stronger and more agile than Pete and didn't want him to slow her down.

She wriggled through the tight confines of the obscure passageway, maneuvered over a support housing, and then shimmied through a sluice bridging the Old East side of Impervious to the upper class West Wing.

Because of her social standing, OE had been her official stomping grounds. She preferred hanging out with Eastsiders to the high-ranking gamers, political superiors, and First-Gen money holders that lived in the west wing anyway. As a matter of fact, even when moving through the guts of the city, Fran typically made it a point not to wander outside of her old east neighborhood.

From the east side, however, the only venting to the surface floor involved a perilous journey straight up a long shaft. Chan had been the only one she'd known to make that climb. The west wing ventilation system, however, had recently undergone renovations and now boasted a step-like configuration — apparently to allow for a fresher air-flow or something.

She took a deep breath and noted the luxurious aroma, like fresh flowers and cinnamon, maybe. Shaking her head, she continued moving upward. As long as it made her climb easier, she could care less what kind of air the snobs choked down. Of course, had she been Accountable, she could have taken an easy ride in the elevator from the sixth floor to surface level.

Whatever.

Notches lined the metallic walls every few feet, allowing for a handy foothold. Fran pressed her hands hard against the bulwark as she climbed three vertical steps before the shoot zigged to a horizontal tunnel. She scurried through, happy for the short reprieve, before the shaft zagged, again, straight up again for another five or six feet.

As light penetrated through occasional mesh covers, Fran caught glimpses of the trendy pods. She paused at each opening to take in the sleek designs. Most sat empty, as occupants carried on their distracted life of opulence. How ironic. The nicer the digs, the less they hung out at home. Fran snorted and began a clumsy scramble forward. The metal walls vibrated with her blunder, and a flash of red shot through the living area of the pod.

An automated voice rang out. "Motion detected. Intruder suspected."

A moment later, a wide-eyed femme entered the living space.

"Hello?" Her voice shook. "Is anyone in here?" With arms extended, the woman turned in a slow circle and tiptoed to the corner of the room to peek behind a low-backed settee. She opened a closet door and lifted mammoth pillows from a sitting-nest. Fran held her breath, afraid the West-Winger might get a little too close to the vent opening. Once satisfied no intruders lurked in the corners, however, the femme stomped over to the sensor panel, swiped in a series of numbers, and exited the room.

Hot breath seeped from the corners of Fran's mouth. Now, mindful of the super-sensitive motion detectors, she slithered past the opening, making a note to use caution at all vent junctions.

The already difficult climb slowed to a snail's pace as she now scaled the venting with softer, unobtrusive maneuvers. By the time she pulled herself onto the landing that marked the surface floor, Fran welcomed the opportunity to give her shaky legs a rest.

Legend said the Ranch lay so close to the surface, Geiger Zombies wandered the hallways at night. The idea seemed laughable, yet pixilated depictions of castoff radioactive humans made more than one kid lose a night's sleep. Bald heads with patchy hair remnants, gaping gum holes, and half-melted faces haunted most nightmares. During her own juvie years, Fran and her friends shared stories of raspy moans, charred lips, and gooey hands, be-speckled with oozing sores. In those days, zombies determined to grab a healthy child in an effort to transfer their radioactivity had been quite believable.

"Melodrama," Fran huffed.

However, a more believable rumor—that poison from the open air permeated the area—could be legit. If so, no one seemed to care since Post Primers were already sounding their death knell.

Visitors and workers were few and far between in these parts, leaving most of the care to automated devices. Graphies greeted the few guests that showed, and outside of the residents, the only real people Fran had seen at the Ranch consisted of hard-luck workers assigned to the hands-on jobs. Like changing undergarments.

The one upside to this cold environment? Fran was able move around unhampered and unnoticed. Even the palm-sized, airborne, RIT's (roaming image transmitters) which buzzed hallways below, didn't fly through these parts. Fran figured the Council didn't have a strong enough stomach to peek in on these declining residents. Her constitution, on the other hand, had adjusted to the sights and sounds.

She peered through the mesh covering marking her exit. In the hallway, a mechanized arm spoon-fed a line of lifeless residents wedged into high-backed chairs. Fran found the thick air, riddled with the scent of the Beast, as hard to swallow as the gloppy porridge that dribbled from the Post-Primers' mouths. Although affronted by the stench, Fran let out a sigh of relief that she had at least completed the climb undetected. She watched the feeding trolley for a few minutes before waving a hand past the beam of light and swiping in the code.

*S*3*4*

Surface floor.

Third hallway.

Fourth opening.

Thanks, Chan.

After exiting, she crept past several pods before reaching Chan's, and then hovered by the opening, almost afraid to peek around the corner—like always. With feet planted and neck extended just enough to allow a glimpse past the metal door frame, she saw the top of the bed, but no Chan.

She took a tiny step forward and craned her neck a little more until she could see the whole bed.

Still no Chan.

After choking back another mouthful of fear, Fran lifted her chin, placed hands on her hips, and stormed into the room. A bluish glow from an old fashioned video display illuminated an empty bed on the far side of the chamber. Outside of the occasional whirring of a nearby food trolley or med dispenser, a hushed silence filled the room.

Fran's heartbeat picked up, and she turned in a slow circle. She must have missed something. *Bed. Video display. Closet.* No Chan.

As she pivoted in the panicked circle, her eyes blurred. *Gray. Blue. Gray.*

No Chan.

"Chan?" She croaked out his name which sounded too loud reverberating through the silence. Fran rushed to the single bed and touched the gray coverlet.

Cold.

Pointed corners created sharp right-angles—a task perfected by a robotic arm—leaving the bed snug and unwrinkled. She dropped to her knees and checked underneath before running to the free-standing locker which housed Chan's belongings, but all traces of her mentor had been erased. The presence of death lurked in every corner. The Beast had moved in.

While holding onto her breath, she backed away. Her leg bumped into the tight mattress of his bed, and Fran fell onto the mattress with a quiet oomph. She scraped the tears threatening to spill. She wasn't going to be like the drama queens who bawled at the feet of loved ones. That's not how a wolf behaved.

She stood and lingered by the bed, her gaze drawn to the depression she'd made on the scratchy covering. She liked the implication. Someone had been here. Someone had cared. The ugly, tight-cornered, scratchy abomination once housed her mentor. It held him to its fetid bosom and watched him disappear. She trembled with emotion, lifted her leg and shot a worn boot into the carcass of a bed.

The metal screeched and the bed shimmied. Fran hopped back, and with lifted fists, switched her stance to unleash a ferocious side kick. Dead on. The bed careened into the far wall.

Her body hummed with rage as she chased the retreating abomination. Front kick, side kick, left and right. Crisp sheets softened and carefully-tucked corners unfurled. The thrill of a small victory belong to Fran as the mattress shook and shifted from her lethal assault. Tiny beads dotted her forehead as if she had transformed weak tears to angry sweat. Fran celebrated the small triumph as she looked upon the unkempt bed. Of course, the mechanized arm would soon return and erase her efforts. But for this round anyway, she emerged the victor.

On a huff, she turned to exit. As she did, Fran could have sworn the ravaged coverlet winked a goodbye. She turned back and moved closer to the bed. A glint of light reflected off a nub sticking out between the mattress and metal frame. She touched it.

Her heart raced.

Seriously? It couldn't be.

Fran pulled the small, shiny rectangle from its hidden confines and brushed the surface. Most residents owned one. It carried the daily news and special events and was used for games, and mail, and all sorts of things. She'd even rented one back in her school days. But this one was different. This was *Chan's* cherished reader. The one he had kept from her view. The one of which he had claimed, *"There's things in here you're not ready to see, Wolf. Not yet."*

But now, he had left it for her.

Right?

Somehow, even in his declined state, he had remembered to pass on the legacy. Fran's mouth lifted into a shaky smile. Chan's final act as the perfect mentor. Dwarfed by the enormity of his action, she hugged the reader to her chest, and felt her heart dance upon the hard surface.

She remained until the silence of the room grew in size and soon the drumming in her chest sounded too loud. A tingle moved through her body, just like when a Graphie was close at hand. However, this presence wasn't of the holographic nature. It heralded a unique malevolence, and it wanted to consume her.

The Beast.

Fran tore out of the room and raced through the hallway. The thought of being spotted by a low-ranking worker never entered her thoughts. The cruelty of the Beast chased her down the hallway as Fran sprinted toward her escape. She had to get away, far away from this place. If the Beast could consume her sharp-edged mentor, Fran knew it wouldn't hesitate to pull her into its decaying embrace. She panted. No, she couldn't even breathe. Her lungs refused to move. Was she dying?

*S*3*4*

The venting hummed and a roar from the Beast's leathery lips engulfed her head. Heat from its breath seeped in through her pores. The grating slid open. She shoved the reader down her shirt and dove for cover.

She zigged. She zagged. Sightseeing forgotten, Fran scurried across the sluice and back into the OE. With movements as mechanical as the cold arm feeding the residents, she pressed on, not stopping until she reached the compartment she called home.

Once enshrouded in her canvas blanket, she closed her eyes and listened to the sound of her own labored breath. The rise and fall of her chest slowed, and the essence of the Beast began to dissipate. When she finally felt safe, Fran tugged the canvas from her head and sat in the darkness rubbing its frayed edges.

The reader poked into her skin and she pulled it from its sweaty confines. As she waved a hand over the power sensor, a glow from the screen lit up her niche as bright as a Light-Genie. She brushed a thumb over various icons which held Chan's most prized information. Venting schematics, stats on each Rebel, black-market movies, communication software, and at least twenty other random folders stood at the ready. Her eyes darted around, her thumb eager to brush over each and every icon.

She swiped a folder labeled *Diary of a First-Gen* and after a quick blip, words appeared on the screen.

We hadn't heard the missile strikes but instead felt them — vibrations so profound as if the core of the earth writhed in pain. And below the surface, although sealed up tight, undue panic spread among the residents.

Excitement lifted the tiny hairs on Fran's neck. A real first-generation account? Sure, she knew the story of Impervious' beginnings from the mandatory studies in her school days. However, those texts were nothing more than a list of facts weaved together with a few conjunctions to form boring sentences. This account read differently. Like a story.

She held the reader close to her face—too close, probably—with her nose but a few inches from the screen. She'd always loved to read and had gobbled up story after story throughout her era of learning. However, it was all Sanctioned stuff *like The Laws of HAZMAT, The History of the Council, and The Sons of the Generations*. The idea that she'd unearthed a pirated, unsanctioned story gave her goose bumps. And not the kind that Graphies caused, but ones elicited by delicious excitement.

The words of a First-Gen.

Fran—a Fourth Gen, born and bred underground—knew of her lineage. Mom—a Third-Gen Impervieite—lived a similar life to Fran's. Of course, her Second-Gen grandmother was the first round of babies born into the city. But before that? Sanctioned accounts didn't reach back that far. But, this? This account from fifty years ago, by a man who had seen the world before the war? It read like a crime thriller…

Radiation. The mere mention of the word had the ability to send most Impervieites into a fit of unsolicited shivers. To say The War of Annihilation created a nuclear mess would undersell the severity. The political and social climate had come to a boiling point. We knew what lay ahead and had anticipated the complete obliteration of 70% of the earth's land surface would turn the globe into a melting pot of whacked-out weather patterns and radiation fallout.

Even if an above-grounder survived the initial flares, the ensuing radiation sickness, innumerable plagues, nuclear winter, and plain old starvation would have left him wishing he had perished in the blast. However, being academia from the old world, I wasn't one to fall prey to the urban legend of Geiger-ghosts. Radioactive zombies who roam the earth? Sensationalism at its finest.

Having been one of the original designers, I knew every last detail of the containment city. Yet at DEFCON-1, even I had experienced unwarranted dread. Panic sparked gossip, and soon rumors of permeating radiation flooded the bunker, and with them, a tsunami of fear.

But then good ol' Marcus – Head of the Building Council – became the man in charge. He managed to calm the masses like a cup of warm milk. Just a touch over thirty, with a premature sprinkling of grey at his temples, he spoke with authority and kept a level head. Like a courageous father, he led his family.

He exuded authority as he stood on the platform, speaking to the last survivors of the world – the ones who'd paid a small fortune for salvation. His blue eyes sparkled with sincerity as he promised the residents that each and every last one of them would witness the day of rebirth. The Epoch. Even now his words, embedded deep in my brain, reverberate in my ears.

"… And rest assured no one and nothing can permeate this bunker. It's… Impervious!"

But is it really? Just a few years after that great speech, the plague ensued. Like a demon, it stole the minds and bodies from seemingly healthy residents. It made no sense. It had to be the radiation. We fortified our impervious walls with an entire second layer of metal and filled every conceivable minute gap with innovative lead soldering. But the plague continued.

We filtered water with manufactured solar splicing and stored it in impenetrable holding tanks. And yet the decline of humanity raged on. Even food products that had never seen the light of a natural day underwent strict irradiation techniques to squelch this radioactive killer. Yet death gained momentum.

As I write this, the average lifespan has been reduced to forty short years. What will become of the second generation?

Chapter Four

"Come on Pete. We've played *The Mad Hooligan* for hours, and I'm getting hungry."

She shouldn't have told Pete about Chan's reader. In fact, Fran would have kept the secret to herself, had Pete not snuck up on her—*again*—while she slept with the reader hugged to her chest like a favorite doll.

Busted.

She had fallen asleep reading the diary, and now couldn't wait to get back to the story. She'd kept the *Diary of a First Gen* to herself, pacifying Pete with *The Mad Hooligan* when he'd insisted on seeing Chan's secret games. It seemed like a good idea at the time, but now impatience gnawed on her nerves. Pete kept his eyes trained on the reader and continued to manipulate his avatar with one hand while holding up the index finger of his free hand.

"I'm serious, Pete." Fran whipped the reader from his lap, and the game timed-out. She shoved the reader down her canvas jacket and began to crawl away. Pete didn't follow.

Good.

Although she'd warned Pete about waking her, she'd welcomed today's wake-up call. Throughout the night, Fran had wrestled with nightmares of dragon-like creatures chasing her through a dark labyrinth. Then, the terrors morphed from dragons to zombie forfeitures who ravaged her flesh to steal her life. Pete to the rescue? Maybe, but he blew it by overstaying his visit.

Fran wheezed a frustrated breath and coughed a little soot from her lungs as she snaked through the labyrinth. She whooped as she passed Folsom's niche and soon emerged into the Agora.

She hung unnoticed behind an acrylic art sculpture just as a trendy West Winger passed by and pitched a half-empty bottle of infused water toward a disposer. The bottle rested on the edge of the transfer, clinging to its precious life. Either the femme hadn't noticed, or she didn't care. Either way, Fran arose the victor. Her eyes widened, and she licked dry lips. The plastic bottle balanced on the rim of the disposer and she knew one false move could suck it into the vacuum of the waste transfer. She snatched the bottle and gulped the sweet berry-flavored water. With dreamy eyes shut, she reveled in the delicious accident, sucking down every last drop until the bottle ran dry.

She wiped her mouth with the back of her hand, and, following a grunt and a throaty belch, lifted her lids. The passing residents came back into focus, including a few snobs who tsk-tsk'd her objectionable behavior.

Whatever.

As a nearby squawk rang out through the courts, Fran turned to check out the commotion. And then froze.

The crazy body piercings. The garish makeup. The outlandish hairstyle. And riding a *Drag-Racing, Air-Generated, Original Nanocycle?*

Moving walkways, for the super-lazy, lined the perimeter of each housing sector, so nobody — other than city workers or craggy Superiors — rode motorized vehicles. Except, of course, those being treated to an Allocation of Inequity. A night of ultra-decadence and hedonism. A gift bestowed upon the super elite. A reward for dedication to the Council serving a dual purpose: Incite jealousy and encourage submission.

"A-O-I." The words came out on a whisper.

The bottle fell from Fran's grip and bounced onto the floor. She raced to a nearby bench, hopped up and scanned the court. The scooter, otherwise known as the DRAGON, tricked out with high chrome handlebars, spewed a brilliant rainbow from the luminescent exhaust. And Nissa sat upon the steed.

Shrieks rang out from all directions as her sister-in-law circled the court, sans helmet, on the low-riding bike, whipping to and fro. Fran's blood boiled. The careless witch even zipped past a new mother, almost clipping the edge of an electronic buggy without acknowledging the near miss.

And then she spied him. Curls fell about his face, almost hiding his easy-going brown eyes. Her chest squeezed as she remembered his gentle kindness. His classic good looks, as well as amiable smiles and nods, seemed to sooth the victims of his wife's mishaps.

Fran's eyes welled. "Ted."

The thunder of the second scooter sounded close by, and Fran flicked a gaze back to Ted's wife. Although she'd almost rammed her roaring DRAGON into a café table, Nissa tossed her head back and howled with laughter. The café patrons scattered and others ducked and swayed as she whipped around the courts. Although annoyed, Fran used the opportunity to her advantage, pocketing a few table scraps while the dynamic duo entertained the crowd. For the grand finale, they each threw their ride into hover mode and jetted high above the heads of their audience to the awaiting elevator. They dismounted and finished their departure aboard the glass-enclosed lift — up six stories and through the doors of the very ritzy Waltonian restaurant.

Fran heard a few sighs and snickers from the crowd before reverence gave way to chatter, and the court slipped back into its usual state of chaos. Loaded with enough food to slake her greedy appetite, Fran returned to the hidden venting and burrowed into the guts of the city.

As she wriggled through the darkness, she couldn't stop processing the scene. Ted and Nissa lived in the West Wing? No wonder she had never found him. She hadn't bothered to entertain the idea they were over *there*. She inched along, lost in thoughtful annoyance.

After a few moments, when her brain emerged back into the here-and-now, she felt Chan's reader digging into her skin. How could she have forgotten? Prickly excitement tingled the bottoms of her feet, and she welcomed the distraction as she pulled the reader from her jacket. After waving her hand over the surface, she dragged a finger to the image of a green and blue globe—a supposed picture of how the earth looked from outside—her icon for Diary of a First-Gen.

I stare at the calculations on the screen. It's safe out there... It has to be safe. I toggle over to the latest readings. Gamma rays, alpha particles, beta particles... the numbers all line up. Yet without a doubt, the Quality Factor Reading is not even close to the safe level. It's been over twenty years in this bunker. How I yearn for the aroma of fresh cut grass on a warm spring day. Yet, I can barely recall the scent of a single blade. Will I even live long enough to see the re-emergence?

We hadn't anticipated being down here more than ten years. And the longer this bunker remains our home, the more bells and whistle Marcus creates to keep the masses happy. Every time we blast through another chunk of the earth to make room for more residents, we seem to discover more building material. Of course, it was planned that way, but I never really thought we need so much room... or that we'd have so many mineral-rich rocks at our disposal.

We've had many new lives born into the bunker – a second generation of inhabitants. Some are already calling their children Second-Gens, as if there will be more. Yet the number we are able to house at this same level of opulence remains to be determined.

Recently, I thought on my days at MIT, twenty-something years ago. Back when I had two trains of thought: Beer and nuclear disasters. I was the designated beer-guy. At the liquor store checkout, I had felt cocky and told the cashier that I was crashing an AA meeting. She gave me the stare of death until, with the smugness of youth, I added, "I meant, Apocalyptic Analysis, ma'am." We thought we were something back then: The few… the proud… the physics geeks.

Science club may not have been a popular after-school activity for most, but we, fascinated with the idea of nuclear catastrophes, had spent hours of free time tinkering with apocalyptic disaster mock-ups.

We had saved mankind and rebuilt the earth with great success several times. Of course, over the years, as we moved through our undergrad and then graduate studies, we created more complex situations. Nonetheless, no matter the consequence, a decade had always been the longest cooling-off period before the rebuilding phase.

Now, here I sit in real time – Second Generation Post Apocalypse – without an end in sight. I'm the last Mohican of the original AA's. I often wonder if I will ever smell the summer grasses again.

Fran blew out a breath and reached into her pocket for a few of the scraps she'd yanked from the café tables. She felt sad for the author, knowing he never had the chance to smell the grass again. Then again, what if she never had the chance either? The reader dimmed with inactivity and Fran sat in the dark for a long moment burdened with melancholy.

Her thoughts bounced between the anonymous First-Gen and her brother. Did she despise Ted, or did she just feel sorry for him? She wasn't even sure anymore. Emotions, once so easy to separate, now converged into globs of darkness and shafts of light.

Her brother was alive.

Her brother was a sellout.

Anger and disappointment had long ago woven together into a dark cloak Fran often tossed over her naked shoulders. Fear and loneliness combined to create a snarky mask she didn't like to peel away. Sarcasm painted any light in her life a dark color, and joy? Pretty much packed up and moved out. Of course, she still clung to hope, but every day even that thick lifeline frayed a little more.

Fran wondered about the aroma of fresh cut grass. She had visited a park reproduction once long ago with Mom and Ted. Mom had guarded her credits until she saved enough for the cybernetic outing—Fran's tenth birthday present. The simulated park seemed as real as anything. She remembered laughing with Mom as they chased colorful holographic butterflies while the sensation of a warm breeze brushed past her face. After shedding her thick boots, she'd trounced through lush grasses, enjoying the cool slipperiness between her toes, and plunged her hand into the icy depths of a simulated river. She splashed, swam, and lifted fistful of the water to her lips to taste the sweetness. After a full hour of delights and surprises, just before the scene de-pixelated, a lone butterfly landed on her outstretched hand, tickling her skin with its delicate wings. Although at the time that experience had satiated her curious mind, now she wondered…

Did everything smell right? What about the temperature and the strength of the breeze? Had she experienced the world as a First-Gen would have on any given day? How would she know?

On the heels of that thought, she remembered one of the morbid CyberTrain videos she'd experienced in Advanced HAZMAT. It had been a lesson for her and her schoolmates titled *Realities of the Open Air*.

In a much darker way, it had felt as real as that day in the park. The landscape of her classroom morphed into a mottled-appearing earth with mounds and mounds of ash under a murky gray sky. A cold wind whipped through the air, scattering the dust in a swirling storm, and Fran felt the sting of acrid-smelling flakes.

The head of a holographic man emerged from a hatch-like opening where her teacher's desk had sat. As the holograph climbed into the atmosphere, his eyes grew wide and his hands went to his neck as if he was choking. His skin sagged as he transformed from the image of a young man into a hideous, aged person. Within seconds, the sagging became more intense, and like gelato running along the edge of a crunchy cone, his chin dripped onto his chest. The man roared in agony until a skeleton, with gaping holes where eyes and a nose had once been, stood frozen in his place. Then… *poof*! He disintegrated and joined the heaping mounds of dust. The wind picked up his remains, pulling them into the storm, and Fran remembered a sickness she felt as the computer-generated ashes of the holographic man touched her face.

With vomit in her throat, she closed her eyes, laid her head onto her desk, and waited until the show ended. The intense mock-up, although nothing more than an artistic rendition like the simulation in the park, achieved the desired effect. She and every classmate vowed never to go outside.

Yet now she wondered. Could the earth repair itself to the pre-war state? The idea seemed as far-fetched as her day in the park. Yet this guy—this First-Gen scientist—thought so. If still alive today, he'd have seventy or eighty years under his belt. Fran laughed at the thought. No one, except Superiors, lived that long. And since Superiors didn't write black market tales, this guy remained just a cool piece of history, as lifeless and dried out as the ashes in the storm.

Too much thinking made her brain hurt, and she paused to rub her temples before reaching into her front pouch for a water packet. She sucked down the contents in a huge, hearty slurp and then waved a hand over the reader.

When the device came to life, a huge skull-and-crossbones hovered mid-screen. She knew the Rebel brand and tapped the icon. A welcome screen morphed into an E-vite to an all-nighter. She sighed and considered her options. Nope. She just wasn't in the mood. She hit the "decline" box, and laid her head onto the hard venting floor, closed her eyes, and tried to imagine what the earth would be like when the Epoch came. Would it be like the movie she'd seen or like what this First-Gen described? Her thoughts faded, and sleep took over.

.~.

Fran jerked upright. Her entire body felt stiff and cold. Her heart raced, and breath came in ragged gasps. Was someone there? She pressed her back into the pipe, trying to become one with the metal while warring to hold her breath. She tuned-in to the surrounding sounds. Creaking and moaning—the usual noises of the pipes—filled her ears. The subtle dance of a venting-bug tickled her face. She wanted to brush it away but resisted the urge to move. The muffled sounds of a family in nearby quarters reached her ears. Maybe she had only imagined the intrusion.

But then she remembered what had startled her awake. Ted in a velvety robe. The whisper of slippers. A spasm of death. A nightmare, filled with color and emotion so real…

Fran reached up to brush away the pesky bug, but found no dancing intruder. Just a trickle of tear down her cheek. And a desire to shed a million more.

Chapter Five

An unexpected sob ripped through her throat, and she placed her hands over her face, hoping no one had heard the sound. Clamping her jaw, she ground her teeth until the taste of salty blood filled her mouth and remained in the darkness until she was sure the weakness had departed. After stowing the reader back into the folds of her jacket, Fran rose onto all fours. She crawled and tapped, mentally mapping out her movements. When she arrived at the "T" separating east from west, she hesitated. Before allowing time to put the conscious thought together, her body propelled her along a westward shaft—away from the OE—into the West Wing.

Despite the fact Rebel instincts told her to stay away from the sellout wing, she had to see Ted with her own eyes. Just to be sure. It might take a day, or maybe even a week, to search every living quarter, but she had to bear witness to what she only assumed up to this point.

Had he sold out? Had he turned cold to the notion of hope?

She shook her head in an effort to disperse the nagging thoughts and, like a creepy peeper, stole glimpses inside the residents' personal living spaces. Every pod looked the same with white epoxy-coated floors and matching stark walls. In an effort to mark originality, however, each owner outfitted his little slice of Impervious with artistic sculptures, shimmery wall hangings, and colorful pillows onto the trendy, acrylic furniture. But layouts were the same, each residence equipped with a communication room, kitchenette/living room combo, bedrooms, and spa-like bathrooms.

One couple sat in the com quarter with a trio of Graphies who reported the morning news. Another pod housed a couple still slumbering under a silky coverlet. Smells of fresh coffee and newly-delivered breakfast foods put Fran's belly into a neurotic state of hunger. For a moment, she even considered a quick break 'n' snatch to curb her grumblings.

Every single pod on this side of the city belonged to somebody important. And, as Fran had already witnessed, strict surveillance equipment guarded these prized properties. She knew if she dared open the grating, a Graphie would be on the scene before she could bite into a puffed pastry or swallow a gulp of a frothy latte.

She moved and peeped, gawked and sighed. Blurs of side tables, vases of fresh flowers, video display units, and holographic children's toys filled her vision. Mothers clothed fat babies and stuffed them into electronic walkers while fathers carried readers in trendy side satchels. As people moved on with their day, the living pods began to empty and soon, the West Wing grew still.

Fran continued searching for traces of Ted, knowing she would settle for anything that might indicate his presence in one of these upscale spaces. She zigged and zagged, checking out a portion of each unit with practiced calculation. After hours of tedious peeping and with dwindling adrenaline, boredom began to settle it. Every pod began to look like the next and she yawned as she noted:

Living area, kitchenette, com-quarter.

Living area, kitchenette, com-quarter.

Living area, kitchenette... whoa. This one was different. With hardcore electronics resting on shelves, video screens of varying sizes built right into the walls, and a flagship, high-tech, gaming chair in the center of the room, the space looked more like a gaming chamber than a com-quarter. She discerned faint sounds, like faraway explosions and growls of otherworldly beasts. Maybe the sound of a gaming headset with the volume set on high? Although she couldn't see anyone, the leather chair jiggled, and the metallic clicking of gaming gloves indicated intense tactile maneuvering.

Every Gen-Four considered themselves an amateur gamer. Gaming hubs lined the walls of the city, and minor viewing screens perched on short poles around the Agora. Not only that, readers always carried at least a few games on them. But an entire room *dedicated* to gaming? That smelled professional.

Like anyone her age, Fran knew the big name avatars. Broadcast on the super-screen at the Agora, tournament games manned by the experts pulled in quite the crowd. The last competition between Queen Xyphon and Trekkor II had been a real nail-biter. Fran snorted. Of course, the Queen had won, but Trekkor made a worthy opponent. But because they — pixilated heroes and heroines — commanded the show and received all the glory, no one really gave much thought to the intelligence behind the characters. Fran had never met a pro gamer — not in person anyway.

Soon, the clicking ceased, and the faraway sounds muted. Gloves landed on the floor, a green light surrounded the chair, and a femme's very loud voice filled the silence.

"Hey, can you come here?" The green light blinked twice.

"Right here, Nis."

Nis?

"No, you lazy cretin. I mean really come here!"

"Give me a sec."

Ted?

A moment later, Fran heard the whoosh of an unseen door. The chair whirled around, revealing her sister in law decked out in a white tank and purple Lycra pants that hugged her body like a second skin.

"It's about time," Nissa whined.

"So where's the fire?" The sarcastic comment sounded so Ted. Fran envisioned his lopsided smile — the same smirk he'd always worn when he'd teased her back in the day.

"Sit down. You have to check this out, mate." Nissa's voice trembled.

"Sure. Wow me."

A chair scraped against the floor as the lights dimmed, and much like the virtual experience in her old classroom, the gaming quarter transformed into a rocky, desert-like terrain. Holographic zombies roamed about the room, and although Fran knew Nissa still sat in the gaming chair, both the chair and the master had all but disappeared into the landscape.

Suddenly, the room filled with a deafening roar, and a fanged reptilian-like creature arrived on the scene. Fran sucked in her breath as she looked upon Behemoth—a well-known avatar who'd been rising through the gaming ranks. As the animal stood on its hind legs, leathery wings unfolded from slick, fibrous skin.

Frightening, yet majestic.

Even crouched outside of the pixilated landscape, Fran felt dwarfed by Behemoth's presence and recoiled deeper into her hidden space. Secretions oozed from his nostrils, dripping from the corners of his mouth while his serpentine neck rotated his head a hundred-eighty degrees. Seeming satisfied with the surroundings, Behemoth released one last snarl and took to the sky.

Although Fran had to crane her neck to watch him move about the room, she could see he sailed with the grace of a hawk—quite odd for such a ghastly creature. He gained speed as he soared, and gargantuan claws clattered as he descended low to the ground scraping a boulder. The scene looked so convincing, when he reversed direction, Fran's knee jerk reaction was to duck right before Behemoth spewed a thunderous war-cry and dove into a large rift in the rock.

"MAN DOWN!" The words lit up on a large video display, followed by the status of Queen Xyphon and Behemoth. Even score. An electronic voice permeated the speakers.

"Five-minute time out."

Realizing she'd been holding her breath, Fran exhaled. The landscape faded. The yellowish glow of the room transformed to a bright luminance, and Nissa swiveled around.

"So? What do you think?"

Fran pressed her cheek onto the mesh just like Pete, hoping to get a glimpse of her brother. A moment later, Ted moved into view wearing a pair of canvas trousers similar to Fran's along with white mesh vest. His clothing sported half a dozen pockets housing a myriad of hand-held gadgets. A ringlet dangled over his left eye, and his mouth rested in a lopsided grin. He sauntered toward Nissa in silence and loomed over her chair as if his emotions had tongue-tied him.

His wife stood with a catlike stretch and wound her fingers through the stray curl before she brushed Ted's cheek with generous lips.

"What do you think, Teddy-Bear?" she purred.

"Such a lovely beast." Ted's gentle voice held a wealth of emotion. "And to be honest, I'm grateful the world has no idea what a knockout *my* Behemoth is." He paused and gazed at his wife. "So, are we ready for the *real* Queen?"

"You bet I am." Nissa tossed her head back and let out a whoop, morphing from a purring kitten to gloating lion. "I smoked that old woman!"

"Old woman?" Ted's amusement rumbled from deep within. "For all you know, she is a ten-year-old boy."

"No. I know my players, Ted. She is definitely a fully grown queen." Nissa lifted a brow, and her nostrils flared. "And I've got her number."

"That's the spirit to take into the game tomorrow, Nis."

"Can you believe your wife made it to the stage, mate?" Her whisper reeked of standard Nissa melodrama, and Fran had seen enough. She knew where they lived, so she could always come back. For now, however, she had to either get out or get sick.

As she shimmied backwards, the zipper of Fran's boot caught on a screw. She gave a quick shake of her leg to release the hold.

Bad move.

Her toe hit the pipe and the reverberations caught Ted's attention. His eyes shot to the vent opening and locked onto Fran.

Chapter Six

Fran didn't bother with a quiet getaway. Instead, she scampered through the pipe leaving a wake of vibrations as an automated voice sounded off the intruder alert inside of Ted's pod.

Did he see me? Ted wouldn't betray me, would he?

Even if Nissa notified the authorities, Fran figured she'd be back on her old turf before security arrived. Nevertheless, even after crossing into OE, she kept a stealthy pace, tapping and mapping with one side of her brain while the other side managed her emotions.

Nissa? A pro gamer? No wonder they live on the West side. For some reason that fact made Fran hate her sister-in-law even more. *She'd* stolen Ted from the OE. *She'd* turned him into a sellout.

Fran grunted and shook her head. Her brain ached as if every spongy cell of grey matter had been stretched beyond capacity. She welcomed the darkness as she snaked toward her sleeping niche. Maybe tomorrow she'd read more of the first-gen diary, but right now, she just needed to power down and shut the world out.

.~.

"Come on, Wolf," Pete begged in his usual annoying manner. "It'll be fun. And I bet with everyone watching the big screen, we'll be able to snag some great chow." He tugged on the end of a dread with a gentle, "Toot-toot."

Fran smacked his hand away, as she swallowed a mouthful of hard cheese. Pete had been kind enough to wake her with a miniature slice of cold pizza, so she didn't feel right asking him to leave. Then again, watching the tournament today ranked somewhere below slow dancing with a Superior.

"Not in the mood, Pete. Besides, remember last time? The sour smell of the Council wafted down from their viewing loft, and the whole Agora smelled like old cabbage."

"Whew!" Pete held his nose and waved a hand in front of his face. "Eau de Cronies!"

Fran fought the urge to laugh. Doing so only encouraged his annoyingness.

"Come on, please?"

"No. Go on without me, Pete." She held up the last bite of pizza. "But, bring me back something more to eat, would you?"

Pete cocked an eyebrow. He excelled at facials and arched one eyebrow high on his forehead while the other dove down toward his nose. Sometimes he'd even flip from left to right brow, adding a whipping sound through his teeth... just for laughs. This time, however, Fran could see he disapproved of her request.

"What?" She acted oblivious to her rudeness.

Pete maintained the eyebrow-pose and then, with precision and ease, lifted the top one a little higher. "What's it worth?"

"Whatever I got." Fran held up the crust of pizza. "Although grateful, this scrap only whet my appetite." She dropped her brows and hugged the reader to her chest. "Except for this, of course—not for sale."

The corner of Pete's mouth lifted to join the extended brow. "How about--" He somersaulted away and maneuvered until his back was to Fran. Then, he wrapped his arms around his midsection and exposed his hands to look like those of another person. He wiggled his head and added obnoxious kissing sounds.

Unsophisticated.

Gross.

Fran refused to answer. Pete wasn't her type. He was a clown. Hardly the stud. Then again, if he brought back food… She let out a sigh.

"One kiss."

Pete whooped and rolled back to where she sat. He scooted into her personal space, but Fran held up her hand.

"*First…* bring me the goods."

He chuckled as he inched backwards. "Wolf, when you see what I bag for you, you're going to beg for the biggest smooch ever."

"Great, Pete. Wow me." She added an eye roll and waved him off. Once he slithered out of sight, Fran momentarily considered the big game in the Agora. She snorted and rolled her eyes into the darkness before waving a hand over the reader. While nibbling last bit of crust, she continued reading.

Twenty-two years underground and I managed to persuade Marcus to head up a scouting mission. He said it was suicide. I convinced him that, with the proper outfitting and breathing apparatus, we'd have no reason to fret. He agreed. Although somewhat reluctantly.

Only one exit portal exists and for good reason: The Psychology of Captivity. Because of our innate compulsion to escape anything our brain defines as confinement, humanity wouldn't have been able to resist a doorway. Obviously, a mass exodus before assuring safe air quality would warrant extinction. Therefore, outside of Marcus and myself, no one knows how to get out. Does it sound heavy handed? Perhaps now it does. However, due to the catastrophic political climate of the earth at that time, anonymity was a minor demand and readily agreed to by each patron as they were blindly ushered in to their new habitat.

I have an odd feeling about the mission. You know, like when you feel like someone is holding back info, but you can't quite put your finger on the cause? Anyway, Ema, Second-Gen botanist, will be making the trek. Am I worried for her safety? Not really. Ema's made up of brick and mortar. She'll hold up just fine.

Fran leaned against the hard, metal wall. The reader dimmed to sleep-mode as she considered the idea. An exit portal? The History of Impervious always taught that the city was sealed, soldered, and reinforced from the inside to keep citizens safe. The History of Impervious had always taught that when the Epoch arrived, the metal dome that made up their air-tight silver sky would be demolished using diamond tipped drills and high efficiency laser slicing.

But *this*… This idea of a doorway leading to the open air. The concept both enlightened and frightened her, and her heart drummed with anticipation, eager to unlock more mysteries within the rest of the story. She waved an impatient hand over the reader to wake it from sleep mode. Every fiber in her body hummed as she waited for the glow to illuminate her niche. "Come on." She urged the reader with a shaky hand, but it remained lifeless. She waved her hand again and waited.

Nothing.

Seriously? She needed a charging station… pronto. She stuffed the device down her shirt, and started toward the Agora, but soon halted.

The Game.

The Agora would be flanked with thousands of game-watchers. An available charging station would be next to impossible to find. Not to mention, Security Graphies would hover in every corner. Fran moved back to the niche and leaned into the pipe with a disappointed sigh. As she sat in the darkness and chewed on her lip, she considered where the portal might be located. She had branded the schematics of the entire ventilation system in her head, but she had never committed a map of the entire city to memory.

It only made sense that the portal would be at the Surface. Armed with that theory, she eliminated floors eleven through one. Fran did some quick calculations in her head. Because the diameter of each floor measured two miles, the radius would stretch a mile. With the aid of good old Archimedes, Fran deduced that the area of the floor be as simple as Pi; 3.14 square miles.

I'm such a geek.

She smiled and reflected on her school days remembering the look of surprise on Professor Englehardt's face when she garnered a perfect calculation for the *Collision Impact Rate of Plasma Energy*. Freddie, her annoying nemesis, had whispered "geek" from his seat behind her in class. That, of course, made her cheeks heat up, but the project had garnered her an "A." After another rude comment from Freddie, she proceeded to tell him to knock it off or she'd use the calculation on his face. The moron must have figured she could do it, because it shut him up. Definitely wolf-in-training. Whatever.

Fran pictured the graph in her head and decided to slice the Pi into quarter-mile square plots. Once she felt confident of the layout, she overlaid the venting schematic in her mind's eye and visualized the two together. No doubt, she had a lot of ground to cover, but what the heck? What else did she have going on?

Closing her eyes, she allowed her brain to focus and brand the diagram into her frontal lobe. She opened her eyes and released the memory before closing her eyes and pulling up the drawing, allowing her mind's eye to 'see' it again. This time, she held the vision while tapping her finger on the metal floor.

Open eyes, rinse, and repeat. Fran continued the training until she could 'see' the mission diagram with open eyes. A short while later, she scurried off to make the trek to the surface level, employing the same passage used just a few days ago when she had gone looking for Chan.

Being that the Ranch took up most of the surface floor, it was the most logical place to start the search. However, her stomach churned with fresh memories from the last outing, and the stench of the Beast filled her senses.

She zigzagged through the step-like concourse, stopping midway to catch her breath on the sixth floor landing. She closed her eyes for a brief reprieve, and rubbed her lids. Her eyeballs always seemed to burn or itch. Perils of a Rebel. As she luxuriated in the moment, Ted's face blossomed in her mind and she remembered how he would make up stories for her when they were kids. On nights when she couldn't sleep, he, being the older, smarter brother, would fashion a picture of the new earth. He'd talk of butterflies and soft green grass, and after a while, she would drift off to sleep.

Fran snorted at the last picture of him in the gaming chamber sporting gadgetry in his shirt pockets and drooling over his idiot wife. *Seriously bro? A sellout?* Fran blew out a hard breath, enraged by this new version of her brother. *That's it. I'm going to give him a piece of my mind.*

Turning away from the climb, she took off through the diagonal shaft leading to his neighborhood. As she moved past the gaming chamber, the roar of Behemoth blended with the whistle of a rocket launcher. Good, Nissa was still manning the game, which meant she wouldn't get in the way. Fran's stomach got all tingly thinking of Behemoth, and she cursed herself for caring.

Moving forward, she peeked into the next room. The simplicity of the décor surprised her. She thought for certain Nissa would be all sparkles and glam, but it actually looked tasteful. Did she dare say cozy?

Ted sprawled on a lounger with a reader in his lap. He looked so comfortable. So at peace with his life. A feeling akin to homesickness wafted through her insides—warm, but painful in a longing sort of way. She watched him and let the gnawing fester. Before she knew it, memories of Mom flooded her soul—not specific outings, or even mind pictures, but recollections of happiness and joy. Feelings so deep she thought she might drown, so bright they could blind her if she looked into their center. Before she could even begin to paint them with sarcasm and darken their luminescence, a knife tore through her core. She clapped a hand over her mouth to shut out all sound, but a sob launched from her depths and shot right through her fingers.

Tears of weakness spilled from her eyes, making her wonder how long they'd waited on the precipice. With her mind trapped in a morass of emotions, she didn't think of the danger as her brother's name rolled off her tongue.

"Ted."

Her voice came out choked and raspy, but the sound was enough. His head lifted.

Fran brushed a hand over the light and configured her whereabouts—sixth floor, second hallway, fourth pod. The holographic key pad danced in front of her eyes, daring her to swipe the code.

*6*2*4*

The cover lifted. Ted leapt to his feet. Fran slithered through the opening. He waited three steps away. She jumped onto the epoxy coated floor. His arms opened wide. She stepped forward, and he pulled her into his embrace.

"Wickworm." He whispered her childhood name, and she smelled his sweet cologne. So afraid to lose the moment, she stood unmoving, eyes closed, and listened to every beat of his heart. She would have been content just to take in Ted's essence and draw from his strength but soon felt a buzz in the air.

Her skin prickled. A current of power flooded the room. How did security already know? Were the trendy pods equipped with 24-7, big brother surveillance?

"Ted, I can't stay." She peeled herself away from her brother. The air became prickly with the static electricity that preceded the arrival of a Graphie, and Fran ticked off the twelve seconds in her brain. She moved back two steps and watched his face. It read like a story book of emotions: confusion, love, fear, and anger, all bottled up into one goofy expression.

Down to nine seconds. A tingling sensation rippled down her spine.

Five seconds. She reached for the opening, scrambled up the wall, slithered into the awaiting cavity, and waved a hand over the sensor.

*6*2*4*

The venting slid shut, and Fran watched as a holograph pixelated. The Graphie flashed red into Ted's iris and then meandered to the corners of the room. Ted stood in the center of his pod with a confused, tortured expression.

After seeming satisfied with the situation, the shimmering holograph abated, but Fran remained for an extra moment to watch her brother and his funny look.

Chapter Seven

Why did I do that? Fran cursed her actions and caterpillared backwards. Chan always warned against this careless type of action. How had he phrased it? Something on the order of *"Be vigilant, Wolf. The old Fran is still alive in there somewhere."*

She continued to chide herself all the way back to the zigzagged venting and for the entire next floor of her ascent. By the time she climbed up to floor four, however, her brain had quieted. She refocused on the upward movement and her original task. Near the surface, the smell of the Beast entered the shaft, and panic prickled her senses. Irritated with another wave of weak emotions, she pressed harder into the side of the flue, jamming her toes into the notched footholds. An itchy sweat accumulated on her scalp and spread down the back of her neck as her legs hummed from the exertion.

At last, she flopped, belly-first, onto the final landing and took a moment to rest before reaching through the grating to apply the code. The covering slid open. She crawled out, stretched her back, and resisted the urge to sneak over to Chan's old room. She scanned up and down the hallways hoping to see something that would offer a clue. She snorted. What did she expect? A lit-up sign that said "Open Air" with a thick arrow to point the way?

As Fran contemplated which direction to go, she wondered how she would recognize the portal. Would it look like any other door—a sleek slider with a sensor panel to the left? Maybe it would be an enormous wheel made of steel that she'd have to crank to release the hatch. It might even resemble the pictures she'd seen of old fashioned doorways with a shiny, rounded knob at the height of her belly-button. She leaned against the wall, closed her eyes until the plotting map blossomed into focus, and then hurried to the first room along the hallway.

Point A. Identical to Chan's. Single bed with tight corners, old fashioned computer, and haze-gray locker standing open, devoid of contents. Fran examined the ceiling, scanned the walls, moved the locker out of the way, and then checked under the bed. No trap doors. She rapped her knuckles up and down the wall and listened for any sign of hollowness. Nothing.

She moved on to the next room—Point B. Similar to Point A. When she opened the steel locker, however, a few heavily-stained, wrap-around smocks hung on the hooks. Fran recoiled from the sour smell, and moved across the room to check for any sounds of a hollow opening. As she stood with her ear to the wall, angry voices erupted in the hallway.

"I'm not doing diaper duty this time. I did it last time."

A brief pause followed. A second voice chimed in.

"Hey, how many accidents has the idiot logged this week?"

"I've recorded four, maybe five," the first guy responded.

"Yeah, that's what I thought. You know what that means?"

The first guy let out a whoop. "End of the line, buddy!"

Fran winced at the careless laughter that came from the two.

"Yep. So long sucker."

"Come on; let's get our drink on with Freddie."

Fran tiptoed to the doorway, peeked around the frame, and spied the backs of two uniformed guys as they moved away. They walked with the swagger of youth, in no big hurry to complete their job. In the middle of the hallway the deserted Post-Primer remained forgotten in his chair.

On a shiver, Fran approached the chair. Stale air surrounded the Post-Primer and she cupped hand to cover her mouth and nose and then looked into the face of the... *Man? Woman?*

Those being cared for at the Ranch wore similar smock-like tops and wrap around pants, dotted with chunks of gloppy porridge. Sharp shoulders, elbows, and knobby knuckles jutted out at odd angles as if they might burst through the confines of paper-thin skin. Eyes reflected yellow where the white should have been, and a murky gray-blue through the center. They seemed to lock on to Fran, with a silent plea for help. The Post-Primer lifted a gnarled hand and drew pasty lips apart, just as a new set of voice bellowed from around a far corner.

"Come on, Bullwinkle. Let's get this job done so we can head out for the day."

Fran took one last look at the boney face, mouthed the word 'sorry,' dove into the nearest room, and lingered just the inside the threshold.

"Where do they take them anyway? Ya know, after we drop them off?" This guard sounded just a little younger than the first.

"Who knows? Who cares? I'm figuring an incinerator of some kind. Less mess that way."

Fran grabbed her stomach. *Don't go there, Wolf. Stay above it.*

As much as she wanted to find the portal, an even greater need to depart from the lair of the Beast pervaded every living cell in her body. Fran waited for the sounds of the guards to retreat before slinking back to the venting. Within a few short hours, she had learned about an exit in this buried city, shared a mini-reunion with her brother, and stared into the murky-blue eyes of a resident who warred with the Beast. All she wanted to do now was chow down and sleep.

However, when she remembered her promise to Pete, a new burden weighed her down. She wouldn't call Pete's kisses awful. His lips felt soft and warm, and his breath tasted like sweet cinnamon candies on their last encounter. However, if the scenario played out anything like the last time, the kiss would give him false hope, and a hovering, love-sick Pete-shadow would annoy her for the next several days.

She zigzagged down the chute and then paused on the sixth floor platform to give her shaky legs a moment of rest. As she rested, she peered over to the diagonal leading to the second hallway of the sixth floor.

No. Don't you dare, Wolf.

Too late. She scurried toward Ted's place. *Just a peek.* She moved past the quiet gaming chamber without even glancing inside knowing the match would be over by now. As she continued to crawl, her knee bumped into something.

What the…?

As soon as Fran reached down, she felt an aluminum meal carton. A heavy, warm, aluminum meal carton. She ripped off the top and hot steam, laden with the savory aroma of burgers and fries, wafted across greedy nostrils. Her stomach ripped a ferocious roar while a shiver raced through her body. Salivary glands lubricated her mouth, and her taste buds quivered at the delicious prospect. Fran couldn't help but laugh at her physical response as she shoved a fistful of fries into her awaiting chops. Crispy on the outside, gooey on the inside, salted just right, and hot enough to sear her tongue. She forsook all social graces in the dark tunnel, and before swallowing the first mouthful, she attempted to cram in more. She lifted the burger from its aluminum nest. Hot juices drenched the bottom bun and transformed it into a soupy sponge. With the fries squirreled into a fold in her cheek, Fran chomped off a bite so large it hung half out of her mouth as she chewed its meaty goodness. Was that cheddar? Yes it was. And ketchup. And mustard. *And* pickles! Fran ate and ate until she couldn't eat any more.

One burger, hundreds of fries, and a chocolate chip cookie later, she lay on her back and rubbed her swollen abdomen, stretched beyond its norm. After a few minutes of enjoying the most satisfying pain she could remember, Fran rolled over onto her belly and let out a whopping belch before pushing up onto hands and knees. She shuffled backwards with awkward movements and inched past the gaming chamber. As she glanced into the confines, she found herself face-to-face with her brother. His cheek pressed against the mesh, and with the weave imprinted, he bore the essence of Pete.

"Did you enjoy dinner?"

Fran cleared her throat. "Mm hm. Thank you."

"Are you ever going to come home?"

Fran froze and her heart ticked off the seconds of silence. She wanted more than anything to be a family. She missed him more than she cared to admit. But he had deserted her. He had run off with Nissa, leaving no room for a little sister. She continued to back away with no answer for her brother.

Chapter Eight

By the time Fran made it back to her niche, she had digested enough of the food to feel comfortable again. She trekked blindly, but with ease, until she tumbled headlong into a body.

"Who…?" she whooshed out.

"Wha?" A familiar voice replied as warm hands steadied her.

"Pete?"

"Hey Wolf! You're back." Fran could hear a smile in his voice.

She fumbled around for her old Light Genie and soon a soft glow illuminated Pete's sleepy face complete with a cocky grin in the center.

"Brought you some food."

Her stomach recoiled, but she figured she ought to fake gratitude anyway. Pete might have employed some risky maneuvers on her part.

"Oh, um… great. Thanks." She forced a smile.

Pete searched around in his pockets and fished out a worn, but rather large, baggie. He held up the prize.

"Care for some chocolate covered peanuts?"

Fran reached out to take the treat, but Pete snatched it back.

"Not so fast." He scooted closer.

How could I forget?

Although in an awkward position, he managed to nestle up next to Fran and exhale a chocolaty breath in her face. Fran turned her head to offer Pete his prize, but he didn't lean in right away. Instead, he reached over and cupped the back of her head. Fran froze as he moved his thumb in easy circles at the base of her skull. He still reeked of the Agora—a mixture of fried foods and humanity. Fran sensed a layer of men's cologne hidden within Pete's bounty of smells and realized he must have gussied up for tonight's event from a display counter. *How sweet.* Her heart kind-of mushed for his obvious puppy love.

She didn't resist when he pulled her close. In a way, his nearness brought comfort, and her shoulders relaxed for the first time that day. His hot breath on her ear tickled as he whispered her name.

Not Wolf.

Not Fran.

But her real name…Sarah. The name she swore off during her schooling years when her sixth year teacher mortified her by proclaiming that Sarah meant "Princess." Her classmates had giggled until her face burned. From then on, she had become Fran. But now, as the name floated from Pete's lips, enveloped in a hot whisper, it transformed her. The darkness of the day vanished. A flicker of youth flashed through her soul. Their lips touched—just barely—with a sliver of a breath still between them. Somewhere in the moments between the peanut exchange and their merging breath, something changed. For a fraction of a moment, the clown turned into a hero. She pressed into Pete's warm mouth. The cologne, the breath, and a warm sensation in her belly overwhelmed her senses.

His grip tightened on her head, and as he slipped a second arm around her back, her dreads tangled in his fingers, jerking her head back. Pete mumbled a quick, "sorry," as Fran came to her senses and pulled away.

They both remained silent.

Finally, Pete cleared his throat. "Okay... Well... Um... Here you go."

He thrust the bag in Fran's direction. Just as her fingers curled around the plastic, he tugged it, along with Fran, toward him. She released the sack and pressed her spine into the cold metal of the pipe.

"Um, you should go, Pete."

An uncomfortable silence hung between them.

"Hey, I was just kidding, you know." He tossed the bag to Fran, and shimmied backwards. His loud voice amplified off the surrounding metal pipe. "I mean, this guy knows when to leave well enough alone."

Fran heard a 'thud' and looked up to see Pete rubbing his head. He mumbled a few curses and moved outside of the glow from the Light Genie. His strained voice rang out from the darkness.

"So, I'll see you tomorrow?"

Fran allowed a tiny smile to inch across her face.

Chapter Nine

After giving Pete ample time to scatter, Fran tucked the reader into her jacket and headed to the Agora. The post-game, semi-deserted courts lacked the typical bustle. Outside of some leftover gaming wannabes who huddled around the small screens and a few service workers on litter patrol, a small stream of residents trickled around the periphery. Fran sashayed to a charging counter and did a quick shoulder check before pulling the reader from its confines and sliding it onto an energizing pad. She ticked off the seconds in her head and flicked her gaze between the power indicator on her reader and her surroundings. Her skin prickled as a Graphie hovered near one of the small gaming boards ID'ing each of the amateur gamers.

Fran remained on high alert. A nanosecond after the ping indicated a complete charge, she swiped the reader from the pad, and stowed it back into her jacket, while moving toward the nearest vent opening.

Once tucked into the darkness she let out a sigh, moved back to her niche, and before long, the glow of the reader again reflected from the walls of her comfortable cubby. She lay prone, propped on her elbows, with her chin resting on the back of balled fists.

Her stomach growled. *Seriously? Already?*

Like a greedy child, it seemed the more her appetite received, the more it begged. She felt around for the crinkly bag Pete had left behind and then poked a hole through the plastic. After corralling a handful of morsels, she popped a single nut into her mouth and allowed it rest on her tongue, savoring the sensation of the sweet chocolate. Soon the coating melted, and the flavor of the salty nut nipped her tongue. She popped another into her mouth and continued reading.

It's been two weeks. Two weeks since Ema exited through the portal and journeyed into the old world I had known as a child. And one week and six days since her two escorts returned.

Alone.

They say it was cold. That it rained an acid-like substance. They took cover in a nearby cave, and Ema insisted they stay the night. When they awoke, she was gone.

That's what they said.

I insisted we send out a search team. I screamed at Marcus to let me find her, begged him to open the portal. I even threatened to share the secret with the entire city.

He said it was too late. Claimed they soldered it shut this time. But I don't believe him. He's not the same man. An evil seed has sprouted in his soul. A wickedness. A greediness. A desire to rule and control. So what do I do? Where can I go?

She swiped the screen eager for the next entry, but an empty white glow emitted from the screen. She swiped again. And again. The reader mocked her efforts with pale light and a soft hum.

That was it? The end? What about "and we all got out and lived happily ever after?" Or "and by the way, if you want to come for a visit, just click the button behind the empty locker in room fifty-five?"

Why would someone reach into her soul and yank out the newly-planted seed of hope before it had even had time to take root? She wanted to toss the reader down the shaft and into the black abyss before a modicum of reason resurfaced. *What good would that do? Besides, I can still play games and stuff with it.*

Her hands shook, and her mind buzzed. Who was this guy? She wished Chan were here. They'd talk about it for hours, investigate every angle and possible scenario. Together, they would unfold the mystery. Does the exit even exist? Was it soldered shut and hidden away? Did Chan even try to find his way out, or did he fall to the decline before he had the opportunity?

On a sigh, she powered down the reader and nestled into her crinkly canvas blanket to think. Her fingers rubbed the surface, a habit leftover from childhood. The constant touching had worn the fabric, making it soft like old-fashioned cotton. That's what Mom told her anyway.

In the darkness, her mind tracked through the long day. A hard nub bit into her hip, and she felt around under the canvas to locate the disturbance — a chocolate-covered peanut. Pete's goofy smile flashed through her brain, and a shiver threatened her spine, stirring unexpected emotions. Was she ready for this?

Back in fifth grade, she had brought a pamphlet home from school describing what to expect during the *Years of Awareness*. Mom had sat down and talked to Fran about love and kissing and stuff. It had all been very mortifying. Even worse, after the embarrassing conversation with Mom, the next day at school, boys and girls were placed into separate classrooms and the discussion continued with a social worker specializing in the *Years of Awareness*. As a class, they watched a documentary-style video discussing each part of the lip, face, and the various other sensory mechanisms. Every girl had received an anatomically-correct, gender-appropriate plastic doll's head, and for homework, they were encouraged to poke, prod, soothe and even try out a kiss on their silicone friend. They received quizzes and tests, just like any other class. No big deal.

Fran had done fine with the academics even if the idea of kissing a real, live boy terrified her. However, it seemed along with this learning, the rest of her classmates had catapulted into their awareness and couldn't wait to test the waters. She avoided this new wave of activity by staying away from unchaperoned parties and soon forgot about the whole matter—until the day at the Agora when Freddie Stevenson and his posse tracked her down.

They'd followed her around like a pack of pesky Graphies, making kissing sounds and snickering the whole way. The more she ignored the boisterous crew, the louder they became. When she heard freckled-face Freddie announce her as "Sally-Spinster" and "Doll-Lover" from the PA system on the stage in front of hundreds of strangers, however, Fran's simmering temper rose to a boil.

With confidence, she marched up to Freddie and planted a smooch on his lips so intense his face turned bright red. He ran off stammering something about having to get to work. After that, no one tried to kiss Fran again.

Until Pete.

What was it about Pete's nearness last night that had unnerved her? He really did annoy her, right? Never serious, always joking. And what about those crazy eyebrows? She inhaled, remembering the scent of his cheesy cologne. The corners of her mouth twitched with amusement, and that weird feeling returned to her gut. Time to shut down the brain. She sighed and closed her eyes.

Hours later, the need to use the bathroom woke her. She rolled onto her side and lifted up into crawl-mode to make a beeline to the Agora. An angry bladder spurred her on, and she scuttled through the vent in record time. She punched in the code, scurried out the opening, and scampered toward the public restrooms. Because a few cafes remained open, the smell of fresh roasted coffee beans filled the air. The light pedestrian traffic proved to be a good thing for efficiency but not such a good thing for the risk of exposure.

After she relieved her bloated bladder, Fran stopped to do what any civilized human being would do. She waved a hand under the spigot and enjoyed the feel of warm water on cold, achy fingers. A moment later, bubbly soap entered the stream, and Fran scrubbed at the dirt layered onto her skin from the sooty ventilation systems. Did she dare peek in the mirror? Her face might need a good scouring as well.

Fran lifted her eyes, and a Wolf stared back. She moved one hand out of the stream of sudsy water and touched her matted hair. She knew the ends had wrapped together into the ancient style of dreadlocks, but she hadn't realized her once springy curls had all but disappeared into a ragged pile of mange. Soot covered her dirty face, and shifty, blue eyes tracked her movements. In place of her once plump apple cheeks were sharp angles and deep recesses. Her upturned nose now pointed forward, and her neck and jaw appeared more streamlined. In a way, she saw the illusion of her own mother — the way Fran always remembered her before she declined.

Weird.

She scoured the soot from her face, ran her fingers through her hair and tried, without success, to break up the dreads before shrugging skinny shoulders and departing. As she meandered through the Agora, Fran amused herself with the reflection she had just witnessed and laughed at her own double standards. After all, Pete didn't look bad with his thick, wavy hair and deep brown eyes. Actually, the only thing about Pete she found even a tiny bit unattractive were his slightly-bony shoulders.

And he'd kissed her face last night? *More power to ya, Pete.*

In an instant, her brain retreated back to the old sleeping niche, to the glow of the Light Genie on Pete's easygoing eyes. The feel of his breath. His strong hand on her ratty head. Fran's heart rate picked up a few extra beats as she wandered and reminisced.

Lost in her thoughts, she missed the heavy static in the air.

And tingle down her spine.

Temporary paralysis struck like rude lightening, yanking her out of her sweet reverie. She kept her gaze to the floor, yet only a single pair of ratty boots to contemplate meant only a single set of eyes to scan. No time for the paralysis to wear off. No time to find a place to hide.

"In the name of the Impervious Authorities, I request Accountability," the mechanized voice demanded.

For some reason, in the heat of the moment, Fran considered the weirdest thing. *I wonder whose voice they used to create the Graphie commands.* It didn't make sense. Shouldn't she be freaking? Shouldn't she be struggling against the paralysis? Shouldn't she at least be damning the Council in her Rebel head? Yet, instead, this odd thought popped into her mind? Maybe she'd lost it after all. Or maybe she knew.

Her time was up.

Fran lifted her chin and opened her eyes. A red beam flashed in her vision.

"You have been found Unaccountable. By the authority of the Council, you are under arrest...."

She felt Pete's thumb rubbing circles on the back of her head and his breath as he whispered her name. She smelled cheesy cologne and tasted chocolate peanuts. Then her world went dark.

Chapter Ten

"How do you feel?"

Fran lay still, eyes closed, with a throbbing skull. A headache couldn't encompass the sensation—too small of a word for too big of a pain. She didn't know who spoke but also didn't care.

"Shoot me in the head."

It took great effort to get the words to push up her raspy throat and past sticky lips.

"Rebel, your season of unaccountability has ended. You have been entered back into the system."

Graphie or real man? The voice sounded real enough without the audible reverberations of a Graphie, so she placed her bet on the latter. She wanted to peek—just to see—so she peeled heavy lids from her sticky eyeballs and tried to focus on the face. She felt cross-eyed. The room spun. She moaned and closed her eyes.

"It won't take long. Give it another hour or so, and you should feel like your old self."

Old self? Which self? She didn't even want to go there. Especially since her head would soon explode. All over the room. And this strange half-life would be over. She kept her eyes clamped and drifted away.

Before long, a small recognition of sound filtered into her unconscious mind, followed by the glimmer of awareness of her body, which eased into full cognizance of her location. And situation. She opened her eyes. Her headache had ceased. As a matter of fact, unlike waking in the niche, where her eyes would shoot open and a small panic would fill her chest, Fran experienced the feeling of gradual awareness.

To a white ceiling.

And white walls.

Mummified in white sheets, all sanitary and smelling like soap. Fran wriggled an arm out from her freshly laundered confines. A spotless hand boasted neatly trimmed nails. *What?* How long had she been out? She lifted the manicured fingers to her head, unsure what to expect. Soft hair tickled her fingers, and a fine curl brushed over her wrist. *How did they?* She touched a ringlet and enjoyed the light tugging sensation as she combed through the stray lock. But her fingers slipped through to the ends way too soon.

After the third grade, when Mom had taken her to the butcher who had chopped her hair into a babyish bob, Fran had vowed never to cut her hair again. And other than dusting some frayed ends now and then, she hadn't wavered from her pledge. Her hair, although ratty and untamed on last inspection, had touched the center of her spine. But now? Now, as she tried to pull her strands into a low pony, the short curls sprang loose. Her heart thumped as she yanked her left arm free from the sheets. A metal bangle encircled her wrist. Fran swallowed hard to rid the lump forming in her throat.

In spite of the wave of nausea reeling through her body, Fran rose from the bed and moved to a reflective panel on the sliding door. Loose ringlets framed her face like a white puffy cloud. They dangled over her ears and brushed along her jawline. Maybe one or two touched the collar of her gown, but not one reached her shoulder.

The bangle glinted with a sarcastic wink, and Fran realized the device to be a locator. Which meant security would be aware of her every move.

She huffed and her jaw tightened. Her blue eyes held the cold stare of an animal. This fight had just begun.

.~.

A few hours later, after signing on to official Accountable status and re-pledging the Impervious Oath, Fran was released from Holding to her own care, although the bracelet ensured she was never quite alone. So concerned with her well-being after all of the scrubbing and snipping, the Council imparted her with a few credits for clothing and restored her food allowance. Fran licked her lips, eager to do something she hadn't done in a very, very long time.

Although super self-conscious in the skirt they had given her to wear, she felt a strange liberation. Maybe this new status would allow her to sleuth with greater ease. She could even visit the Ranch via elevator. Maybe Accountability could work in her favor. Of course, one small sticking point remained. Fran gazed down at the metal bracelet encircling her wrist and then shrugged. She'd figure something out.

She headed to the hub of the city, moseyed into line at The Lunch Hut, and scanned the menu as it scrolled across a floating screen. Sandwiches with a hundred different combos, salads, pasta, pastries, gelato, lattes...

Before Fran could wrap her brain around all of the choices, a female Graphie appeared by her side, smiling like they always did.

"Hi there! What do you have a taste for today?"

Everything. Fran knew that wouldn't fly, as voice-rec accepted specific menu items only. No chitchat. Instead, she began to recite a list:

"Turkey sandwich on a bun with mayo. No. Make that two... *two* turkey sandwiches on buns with mayo. A large mac'n'cheese. Chocolate milkshake..."

She squinted as the menu scrolled, moving faster than she could process.

"Is that all, Sarah Monde?"

The harsh electromagnescence, coupled with the name the Graphie had employed, elicited a sensory and emotional overload.

A spasm rippled down her spine. "Yes. Thank you."

A red light flashed. "Sarah Monde, you have 10,950 food credits remaining. Please be seated, and your meal will be delivered."

Fran sat at the nearest café table and gazed about the Agora. Same stuff, different day. She looked up the sides of the sparkling walls surrounding the court and counted the floors. *Eleven.* The twelfth floor—the Surface where the Ranch lay—wasn't included in the picturesque cityscape. The vaulted silver dome of a ceiling appeared to be top of Impervious. Although the remarkable feat of architecture hid the shame, everyone knew one more floor sat nestled above the arch. She moved her eyes back to the bustling crowd and sighed. Impervieites sure enjoyed their games of pretend.

Her thoughts were interrupted as the moving treadmill delivered her food. Much like the previous night, her body responded with excitement to the mountain of treats. Unlike last night, however, Fran employed a modicum of table manners. By the time she decided to call it quits, an entire turkey sandwich remained uneaten. Fran stood, tucked the sandwich into the pocket of her hoodie, and moved with the river of residents.

Chapter Eleven

She sat on a bench and perused her bag of new purchases, just a little ashamed of the contentment lingering in her gut. She knew the feeling would be short-lived. A few new gadgets could not squelch her need for freedom. At least she felt more like herself now after ditching the embarrassing mini skirt and replacing it with a new pair of multi-colored Canvies and a pretty cool hooded t-shirt. The Graphie said the color made her eyes 'pop.'

Whatever.

She must have grown over the last year because it clung tighter than her old hoodie. In any event, the new one smelled better. A smile flicked across her face as she looked down at her new boots outfitted with side pockets for gadgets and stuff. She unwrapped a set of newly-purchased wireless buds and tucked them into one of the pockets.

Finally, she heard the hum of a nearby vent opening—just like she hoped. A few knotty nerves rippled as she turned to face the shaft. Pete wiggled through the opening and took a moment to stretch his back before standing to his full height. *Wow, what a bean pole. I guess you just don't notice these things in the shaft.*

As if he could sense Fran's presence, Pete turned in her direction. As a well-trained Rebel should, he kept his eyes to the ground.

"Psst."

Pete flashed a peek her way, and his face lit for a split second before he trained his gaze downward again. He strolled to the bench and scooted in next to Fran.

"I heard about your arrest. Can they really force you to be Accountable?"

Fran tapped her clunky new bracelet onto the bench.

"Looks like I either stay out of the vents or lead the authorities to our hiding spots."

"Well for Pete's sake..." Pete wiggled a brow, but after a moment of silence, realized his joke had fallen flat.

"They cut my hair," she groaned.

"I noticed. It looks good."

Fran's face grew warm, and she snorted, thankful Pete had to keep his gaze to the ground.

"I brought you a sandwich. I'll leave it on the bench."

"Thanks. Do I owe you anything?" Fran envisioned his arced brow. Warmth moved from her cheeks down to her neck.

"Um, I need my reader. Can you get it for me?"

"Of course."

Silence.

"Anything else?"

They both knew what he meant. Fran tried to sound cool. "Bring it to 3-4-2. I'll be there at 1700 tonight."

She placed the sandwich on the bench and walked a few yards before the sea of humanity sucked her into the tide and she moved with the flow.

Where would be a good place to waste some time?

After tiring of the first floor eateries and specialty shops, she swam with the flow of residents up the escalator to the second floor, and meandered to the Spa Art Wing—creative designs for the flesh. She moved past the row of upscale spas whose Graphie-Greeters bragged of their specialty koi ponds and mineral scrubs. *Who would offer their feet to a school of fish and allow them to nibble the dead skin?* Fran snorted and rolled her eyes as she continued through the crowd. Soon, she happened upon a storefront that warranted her attention and headed in for a closer look.

"Welcome to Inked and Linked. Do you already have your design picked out, or would you care to view a catalog?"

The hovering Graphie looked a little disturbing. On one hand, the man spoke with the clear diction and impeccable grammar of an executive. On the other hand, he was tatted and pierced beyond recognition. The odd mix sort of creeped her out. Then again, just about everything in this strange city had that effect.

"I already have a design in mind, thank you."

"Wonderful. Just relax in the chair then. Our artist will see you soon." The Graphie began to de-pixilate, but then, like a person who just realized he forgot one last thing, his luminescence returned. "Can I offer you a mineral water or maybe an herbal tea?"

Fran's laugh erupted with more disrespect than intended. "Uh. No thanks."

She leaned forward in the chair and checked out the floating billboard, just to make sure she hadn't stepped into Le Petite Spa by accident.

Nope. The sign read *Inked and Linked*. However, the tagline underneath added *"The art of saying I do!"*

Fran laughed out loud. She hadn't wandered into any old tattoo domain but one that specialized in the trendy marriage tattoos of Gen-Four. Fran reflected on the femmes she saw in the Agora just a few days prior who displayed their ink like a trophy. Their giggles as they recited the tag line rang through her ears. *"One for him, one for her. An expression of love that fits together like two pieces of an intimate puzzle."*

Nauseating.

A few moments later, a flesh-and-blood human, greeted Fran and copped a squat for the consult.

"So, will your husband be here shortly, or should we just start without him?"

"Sure. Let's just get the ball rolling." Fran enjoyed this role playing a little more than she had anticipated. She shared her ideas with the artist who delved a little deeper to better understand Fran's heart message. The consult lasted about fifteen minutes, and after a few swipes on a QuickReader, the artist created an amazing rendition of Fran's vision, and, oddly enough, her heart.

Haunting blue eyes with cinnamon flecks throughout the gleaming iris stood as the centerpiece. Then, an ever-so-subtle, mere shadow of a wolf mask rested in the background.

It was beautiful.

It was Fran.

She agreed to finish off the piece in the standard wedding-tat with the tail of the wolf coiled around her ring finger. After the art was drawn up and scanned, the procedure didn't take much longer than fifteen minutes from first needle to gauze wrap. Freshly-inked, Fran wandered back into the throng of bodies. The lack of space surrounding her person felt oppressive, and since she had some time to burn before meeting Pete for her reader, it seemed like a good time to check out her new digs.

In a way, the notion of having her own place roused a bit of excitement. Upon ditching Accountable status last year, Fran had still been a minor with no legal rights. But now at fifteen, with legal resident status, she received statutory housing. They assigned her to 336-42.

The ancient woman—like more-than-forty-old—who processed her out of Holding named her "Lucky" because a vacant single had just arrived on the market.

Lucky for me. Unlucky for the resident.

Her old neighborhood with Mom and Ted had been in the same sector, one floor up, so it felt odd and surreal taking the elevator up to the third floor in the OE. When she arrived, a light beam shot into her eyes.

"Welcome home, Sarah Monde." The door slid open. Fran stepped through the threshold of her small studio and walked the length of the pod in no more than ten strides.

Cozy. Open. Nice.

A few molded plastic tables and a flip-flop couch/bed combo rested along the far wall. Tucked away to the right of the living area sat a three-piece bathroom suite complete, with sink, toilet, and shower. *Gee, no steam room? No sauna?* Fran laughed. Compared to her prior digs, this place had the layout of mansion—more than suitable for the short amount of time she intended to hang around.

She sagged onto the flip-flop sofa and released an enormous sigh. She could visit Ted with no restrictions now that she didn't need to enter through the vents, but still felt a weird ambiguity about the whole matter. *A West Winger?*

It could wait another day. Anyway, after a quick meeting with Pete, she needed to dedicate tonight to rehearsal time.

Rumor had it house-arrest went hand-in-hand with community service hours when dealing with Rebel rehab. What, where, and the number of penance hours would be decided at a 10:00 hearing tomorrow. Which played right into her perfect plan. Fran envisioned the probable reactions of the Judges. *They'll be blown away. I'd bet all my credits they've never had a felon volunteer to work the Ranch.* She allowed herself to celebrate the small victory with a flicker of hope.

Until the Beast whispered a reminder of his presence. And the smile ebbed from her face.

Chapter Twelve

Fran peeked into the mirror and fluffed her hair again. Why did she feel so insecure? Pete said he liked the cut, right? But did he? Really? And why should she care what Pete thinks anyway? A quick tingle in her belly answered the question for her.

During the day, she'd stolen several glances at her reflection, just to remind herself what she looked like now, but she still didn't feel 100% comfortable with the girl staring back at her.

Are my lips too big?

She pushed at the spongy flesh. Her bottom lip protruded, and her top lip dipped low in the middle. Curious, she pouted her lips the same way the West-Wing femmes did… But shuddered at the image. *Do not ever do that again.*

She reached into her pocket, pulled out her new com device. The digits read 16:40. She'd told Pete to meet her at 1700.

Close enough.

She strolled out of her pod and moved to hallway four. The neighborhood, set up like a stage around a central gathering place, made it easy to navigate. Twelve separate hallways jutted out from the center, each labeled with clear directional markers. Already in hallway three, her simple journey dictated she follow the markers over one corridor and locate the second venting. She snorted at the simplicity.

The light system worked with old-fashioned motion-activated sensors, illuminating a large berth—ten feet in front of and ten behind—as she moved. The high-intensity glow allowed a view of each doorway she passed. Some boasted a family crest over the threshold to announce their domain. Others tried to jazz up their area with plastic statues and fake flowers. Everyone wanted to be different. Everyone wanted to be the same.

A roving image transmitter, RIT, buzzed past her head. On instinct, she looked down at her feet, but upon seeing her new boots remembered her Accountable status. She lifted her face, and the red beam shot into her iris. An automated voice sounded.

"Thank you, Sarah Monde." The RIT hummed away, continuing its neighborhood watch.

She turned down hallway four and headed toward the arranged meeting place. Just as she arrived, the venting hummed open. Her heart thumped with excitement and she wondered if Pete had been waiting long. As his head popped out, the mesh imprint on his cheek answered her question. A glimmer in his eye made her want to run away, but her feet knew better. They remained glued to the floor as she watched his smile grow.

"Any RITs circling?"

Fran began to answer, but her throat clogged. Though she cleared the congestion, her voice still came out guttural and gross sounding.

"Just one. It's dinner time. I'm guessing we won't see another for five minutes."

"Good." Pete slithered out of the duct and reached inside his shirt to pull out her reader.

"Did you read any of it?" Fran figured he would.

Pete played dumb for almost ten seconds before he sighed. "All of it."

"What do you think?"

For the first time since Fran had known him, Pete wore an expression of concern. "I don't know."

"It's somewhere in the Ranch, Pete. It has to be." Fran held up her bracelet. "I'm going to volunteer."

His brow began to lift. "At the Ranch?"

Fran nodded. "Makes sense, right?"

Pete's standard look of amusement melted into a tender smile. "Brilliant."

Fran moved a step closer until only the reader and the dusty smell she knew so well stood between them. Pete's hand moved to touch her soft curls. She focused on the chocolate warmth pouring from his gaze and moved the last step forward. Her leftover peanuts lingered on his breath.

She moved first this time. A whisper of contentment circled her brain, and the surge of a storm paralyzed her body. She breathed in the dust, tasted the peanuts. Something unrecognizable tugged at her heart and a tear sprang forth and trickled on her cheek.

Pete's rough thumb brushed at the tear and Fran dipped her chin to her chest, embarrassed and confused by her sudden emotion.

On a sigh, he pulled away. "I have to go." He pressed the reader into her hands but hesitated when he noticed the bandage that covered her new art.

"Don't worry about it. I'm fine."

Pete cocked an eyebrow.

"It's just some ink," Fran responded.

"Good. I'll take down anyone who messes with my girl."

With those words hanging between them, she leaned against the wall and watched as Pete crawled back into the guts of the city. Pete's girl? Weird. But then again…

Just as the venting closed, the purr of an RIT buzzed in her ear then flashed red.

"Thank you, Sarah Monde."

The mini security drone took off down the corridor and turned the corner. The sudden silence of the hallway felt way too loud, and Fran hurried back to her room. She moved to the flip-flop, waved a hand past the sensor, and waited for the bed to unfold. Welcoming the thought of mattress under her back, she tumbled onto the bed, kicked off her boots and curled into a ball. After a lengthy sigh, she rolled onto her back and pulled the reader from her side. Nothing new to read since she'd finished the First Gen's diary, so maybe round or two of Mad Hooligan would be a nice distraction.

With a wave, the reader came to life. It appeared Pete had left the Diary of a First Gen open and the frustration over the ending of the story resurfaced. As Fran lifted her hand to swipe the screen, her eyes couldn't help but scan the text. Her hand stopped midair.

What??

She frantically scrolled through several pages she hadn't seen before. What was this? After scrolling backwards through seventeen blank pages, she arrived at the words she read the night prior. Seventeen pages *blank*? Who does that? Excitement rippled through her body like a holograph as she read the new words.

I know how to escape now. I can't say I'm fond of the idea, but I know nonetheless. Am I 100% positive? Do I have proof? No. But I am ready to follow my heart with the hope that it leads me to the woman lost over two decades ago. As of today, I will stop ingesting the clean water that has allowed me to live while others die. As of today, I relinquish the status of Superior. As I write this journal, I'm aware of what my near future will hold. I will become less before I can become more. And, yes, I fear the journey.
To anyone who might be reading these words, I ask two things:

1. *Do not let the fear stop you.*
2. *Pass on the legacy.*

My friend, it is not with the fear of death but with the hope of life that I bid you adieu. And look forward to greeting you on the other side.

Benjamin M. Leiben, Ph.D.

She gasped. Benjamin Leiben? From the history books she knew him as *the* original creator of Impervious. There was even a small statue in the Agora honoring him. However, the history books had always said he had gone mad and, unlike the other Superiors, sunk into the decline. Her head reeled and stomach clenched. So was this all nonsense? The ravings of lunatic? If not, what *did* he mean? If this diary had been written as a means to give her special insight, why did she feel like she looked into a toy kaleidoscope instead?

Shards of color fell and reshaped with no rhyme or reason. How could she make sense of this confusing moving picture that showed the face of an evil leader, a brother who had sold out his hope and lived like tomorrow was promised, and Chan, her fearless mentor, dead from the decline? Then there was Dr. Benjamin Leiben, the Epoch, an exit portal, as well as a missing second-gen botanist. All of the bits and pieces melded together as one swirling mass of information. She tried to pull apart the pieces and examine them each individually. It didn't help. Did she want to cry? Did she want to shout? Both, probably. However, more than anything, she just wanted to shake the kaleidoscope until all of the pieces made a pretty picture. One that made sense.

A quick flip of her arm sent her pillow tumbling into the crack between the back of the mattress and the edge of the couch portion of the flip-flop. She reached her hand through the gap to retrieve her pillow and fished it out, along with a few dust bunnies and a crinkly sheet of paper. Fran looked at the simple, white note with girlish loopy handwriting across the page.

Dear Diary,

I forgot my code yesterday—the same numbers that have accompanied me through life. The numbers that rolled off my tongue as second nature as my own name. Poof. Couldn't remember them at all. Is it possible? Could I be facing the most horrific event in a person's life?

My heart races as I write these words and realize the implications. I had thought I might be one of the lucky ones. That special remnant who would watch the dismantling of our Impervious roof. I had fooled myself to believe I might see the Epoch.

Esteemed forfeiture? I never thought I'd entertain the thought, but what are my options? I remember the face of my mother as she declined, and my heart breaks. I can't do it. I need to take the more dignified path. Tomorrow, I will sign the papers.

A single tear trickled down Fran's cheek. She tried to lock up the ensuing flood, but pictures of Sasha's pinched expression and painful death spasms blossomed under her closed lids. Who knows? Maybe Sasha wrote this note. Then again, Cheyenne the Shy One or any other forfeiture could have written it.

Head throbbing, Fran stood and moved to the kitchen cupboard. She pulled out a dusty glass and filled it from the sanctioned water tin. She lifted the vessel to her lips and sucked down the cool water while remembering Dr. Leiben's last entry… *Sure enough to stop ingesting the clean water that has allowed me to live while others die.*

She contemplated the glass in her hand and felt the rhythm of her blood as it pulsed through her aching brain. Fran counted the beats, knowing they ticked off seconds of her life.

Chapter Thirteen

With the match between Behemoth and Queen Xyphon now just a day in the history books, the entertainment industry stood at momentary lull. Therefore, today's performance— Sentencing of a Rebel—held top billing. In addition to the three judicial members in the shadowed courtroom, the civilian viewing loft teemed with spectators. This audience, mostly made up of the straight-backed do-gooders and ones who couldn't fathom missing an opportunity to wag a finger, eagerly awaited the sentencing. Finger-pointing seemed to feed their self-righteous spirit and mask personal feelings of inadequacy by proclaiming the foibles of others.

But Fran, happy to perform for the group, played the part of a repentant Rebel like an actress cast into the role of a lifetime. Her costume—a crisp button-up, draped with a simple cardigan and complimented by her new, gray mini—seemed appropriate. Humble yet fashionable. She kept her gaze to the floor and hoped her curls would do most of the talking.

Judge number one—a tired looking woman in her early twenties whose expression appeared pained by the tight knot in her hair—spoke first.

"Rebel. What was the reasoning behind your Unaccountable status?"

Fran's confidence this woman could be bought with a sob story led her into Act One.

"My mother. She had declined." Fran's soft whisper had the crowd leaning forward in their seats.

"Say that again, Rebel. And please, use the voice expander provided."

Fran placed the small cube onto the lapel of her blouse. "I'm sorry, Your Honors. I said that my mother had declined."

A stray tear traveled down Fran's cheek and dripped onto her sweater. Soft murmurs and clucking moved through the crowd like a wave. Judge number one cleared her throat. She was allowed one more query.

"And that warranted a breach in your Accountability?"

Her response seemed hard and uncaring—a sentiment that would garner more sympathy from the onlookers in the loft. However, the Committee wanted to see repentance, so Fran responded in kind.

"No, Your Honors. It was foolish."

"Thank you for your candor, Sarah," Judge one finished.

Judge number two— Superior, advanced in age— looked up from a reader. Fran wondered if he even cared about this nonsense anymore. "Rebel. You state your mother declined. Do you have other family?"

"No, sir. I mean, yes, sir."

"Excuse me?"

"Well, my father declined when I was still a baby. However I did—I mean I *do*—have a brother. He married and was on a cybernetic honeymoon at the time of my mother's decline."

"I see."

Judge two looked down at his reader, and a very long pause followed. Had he fallen asleep? Fran bit her lip to contain her amusement. After a few more moments of empty silence, Judge three stepped in.

"And, Rebel, how do you feel penance should be paid?"

Time for her *big number*. Fran envisioned a smoky spotlight and a soft piano playing in the background as she raised innocent blue eyes to Judge three—a nondescript, black-haired nobody. She squared her small shoulders and cleared her throat.

"My heart is heavy because of my betrayal to the Council and my fellow man. I deserve nothing good, yet you found it in your hearts to restore my food allowance and provide me with a new home. I've thought judiciously of how I could repay this debt I owe.

I ask you for forgiveness, your Honors, and request you allow me to serve my sentence on the Surface floor. Allow me to take the job that would bring comfort to those who devoted their lives to our city. I would be honored to be a servant to those who suffer at the Ranch."

A collective gasp rang from the viewing platform. Murmurs rippled through the courtroom and soon escalated to chatter as each voice elevated in an effort to be heard. In a grand gesture, Judge three slammed his meaty gavel. Judge two jolted awake. Judge one wiped a watery eye.

Victory.

"Punishment accepted."

Judge three's rushed verdict made Fran wonder if he feared she'd change her mind. Maybe he was just eager for the gruesome punishment to commence. Whatever. She'd won this battle.

His voice droned on. "…and let this be a lesson to you, Sarah Monde, in the event that your Rebel spirit ever desires to re-emerge…"

Fran stopped listening—her mind too busy formulating the next phase of her plan.

Chapter Fourteen

Fran waited on the bench—the one now designated as her and Pete's meeting place. Her toe tapped an impatient rhythm while she nibbled the ends of her nails. Yes, of course the trip was easier for her than it was for Pete, but that didn't override the impatience she felt. After a short wait, the vent sounded, and Pete slithered out head first. He stood, wiping his pants before coolly wandering to the bench.

"Mini skirt and pocket boots?" He snickered and waved a hand around like a snobbish West-Winger. Fran ignored his attempt at humor and got right to the point.

"I'm working at the Ranch starting tomorrow."

Pete winced and trembled with an overly-dramatic shiver before pinching his nose with a thumb and forefinger.

"Smell you later." He laughed.

Fran blew out an exasperated breath. "You don't get it. I'm going to find the portal."

"Huh?" Pete dropped his hands onto his lap. "It's just… I mean… What about what Chan wrote?"

"Chan? What are you talking about? I didn't see anything written by Chan." Fran shook her head, at a loss for words.

Pete turned to Fran and looked into her eyes. "You didn't see the testimony he added to Doc's diary?"

With his clean face and wetted, mashed-down hair, she suspected Pete thought this meeting constituted a date or something. Fran ran a self-conscious hand through her own hair as a little heat crawled into her cheeks.

Pete cleared his throat. "If you haven't read Chan's notes, there's some stuff you probably don't know yet."

"Like what?"

"Like how to get out."

"So it wasn't all just madness?" Fran felt a moment of relief. Then when she realized what Pete had just said, her heart raced. "Wait. He got out? Chan escaped?"

"Um, sort of?"

Fran didn't like the look on Pete's face, and, even more, didn't appreciate being kept in the dark. She held a mint tight between her front teeth ready to give Pete a verbal spanking.

Then, they both felt it. The static electricity.

"I'm outa here," Pete whispered. He hurried from the bench, swiped the code, and disappeared in less than four seconds.

Fran thought about Pete's words for half a breath and then burst into the stream of residents. She shouldered past a group huddled around a gaming board and past a cluster of chatty femmes. As she rode the lift up to the third floor, she tapped an impatient toe, and upon reaching her residence, raced through the doorway, straight to the flip-flop.

She yanked the balled up blanket from the mattress as she searched for her reader, and located it tucked into the crevice by her pillows. What was her problem? Was there a small piece of her that didn't want to believe? Self-chastisement continued until the reader came to life.

Fran scrolled past Doc's signature line and through ample white space, before she saw her mentor's handwriting. She choked back a sob like she'd been hit in the gut. She remembered how he used to tap his stylus onto his thumb when deep in thought and then tuck it behind his ear between notes. Grief tore through her as she looked upon the meticulous lettering and she ran a finger over the familiar handwriting.

My beloved brothers and sisters,

I know my decline has begun. I must pass along the word to you before I am no longer able. Dr. Benjamin Leiben is indeed a sane man. I knew him well, hired after he lost his sight at the hand of the Council – by order of Marcus – not long after voicing renewed interest in the portal.

Of course, Marcus could have simply finished him off, but as Doc already mentioned, Marcus' soul had turned wicked and his lust for power insatiable. I will not get into the gruesome details of the disfigurement, but I will say that Marcus reveled in Doc's torment.

My children, the Epoch has surely arrived. Indeed, the earth is healed. To date, no one has uncovered the location of the portal, and so we all sit like prisoners in Marcus's made-up world of power. Yet one discovery has led to an escape from this prison. And the decline is the answer.

You see, the Council does not wish to house our sick bodies. Not the weak ones, the sick ones, the hurting, and the lame. So, they place us at the doorway. They think it is our death sentence. Yet, we know it is the beginning of our new life. The Ranch is merely our waiting room, so lift up your eyes and believe. Take heart and rejoice. My brothers and sisters, you may find the journey to be hard, but be of good cheer because I will be waiting for you on the other side.

Every muscle in Fran's body quivered. Every nerve hummed. Did Chan mean that each person who endured the decline still lived? Fran remembered the Post Primer from her last visit to the Ranch. Even if the earth wasn't a swirling heap of ash, he couldn't even feed himself, never mind care for himself in an undomesticated environment. So, how does Chan think they will live?

Faith?

That was the Rebel mantra, right? They stood on the platform of hope, yet, when being completely honest with herself, Fran realized it had never felt tangible or real. More like trying to grab onto a wisp of smoke, a veritable fairy-tale. Had the Epoch represented little more than a symbol for her? A means to defy the reality of her life and justify her anger? Now that the possibility stood before her as a means to an end, she wanted to believe. But it was all wrong—nothing like she'd hoped. And, the very notion of losing *everything* all over again…

Fear sniffed out her weakness—a sensitive heart unable to withstand the pain. That's why she pretended. That's why she'd built the scab. A tear sprung. One weak, ugly tear. She dangled over the precipice of belief, and fear whispered into her ear, *If you pull the scab all the way off, you might bleed to death.*

But hadn't she just learned that good turned out to be bad and death might even mean life? Could that mean weakness might even be strength? Fran pulled back the flimsy covering she had employed to block the voice of fear and looked her enemy in the eye. As she suspected, as the wound reopened, a second tear followed. And then a third. They converged and burned a trail down her cheek, seeping into the corner of her mouth. She tasted the salt and felt the sting of the old mourning and grief.

In a flash, three single tears became a river and the river an ocean as unhealed hurts were exposed once again. The current pulled her in and tossed her about until she was sure she would drown. Could she fight the waves of despair? Would she even be able to stay afloat after having fought for so long?

She stood and paced the length of her living quarters. Her body shook. Every sad goodbye and spasm of death converged into a single mountain of agony. She wrapped shaky arms around her midsection and hugged the pain as it rattled through her body. Soon, she dropped to her knees as the face of her mother appeared in her mind—her beautiful, curly haired mother. The one who had chased butterflies and laughed with Fran until their bellies ached. The one who had nursed her fevers and constructed smiley faces from mundane peanut butter sandwiches. The one who had given her life and cared for the children of Impervious after their own parents were stripped from their lives. The one who had lived in a perpetual place of hope even after losing her own husband.

Fran's body rocked with grief. Sobs erupted as her soul retched, purging the foulness of her sorrow. She cried for the lost years. Wept at the injustice.

Could there be hope? Was there a place where this pain could be turned back around? Was there even the slightest chance her mother might be alive? And what if Chan's theory proved wrong? What if she allowed herself to face the Beast only to be swallowed whole? Could she survive?

Fran wept big ugly tears until her soul emptied of heartache and then she laid her heavy head onto the glossy coated gray concrete. The coolness felt good on her tear-ravaged cheeks. She closed swollen eyes, and her breathing slowed to the shivering hiccups of a child.

After a while, she opened her eyes and stared at the ceiling — a mass of nothing but one tiled square after another. She stared until the pattern converged into a blur of swirling white. Her taut muscles released, and a sigh escaped from her lips. As she became more aware, the back of her hand began to itch, and Fran peeled away the bandage. The eyes of the wolf stared back. Cold, hard blue eyes. Focused and undaunted.

Chan had trusted her with the truth. He had faith that she would move forward. He believed in her more than she believed in her own self. She looked down at the bangle encircling her wrist. Tomorrow, she would enter the Ranch. Tomorrow, she would find her way out.

Chapter Fifteen

The following day, Fran stepped into the Ranch and met with Jan, the Ranch caseworker.

"You've been given charge of four residents, Ms. Monde. Rooms S41-S44." Jan palmed a reader as she ticked off the information. "Most residential care is automated, so your main task is to keep the declining residents company as you tend to each of their unique needs."

Jan turned on her heels. "Follow me please."

Fran clapped a hand over her nose and mouth to ward of the scent of the Beast and scurried along the empty hallway behind the efficient caseworker. They paused in front of a doorway which opened into a closet containing sheets, blankets, and smocks, as well as blue canvas uniforms folded into neat piles and stacked onto metal shelves.

Jan pointed to the uniforms. "Take a set and make sure you are garbed in a clean uniform each day."

Fran pulled a set of scratchy, low-quality Canvies from the pile.

Jan gestured with a smile. "Across the hall is a changing room. You can leave your clothes in locker 22. At the end of the day when you change back into your own clothes, please place the soiled uniform into the receptacle. Tomorrow, you'll come in here for a new pair."

Fran crossed the hallway to where Jan pointed and waved a hand in front of the indicated entry. The portal whooshed open, and she stepped inside of a small chamber containing a few lockers and a single plastic bench. Before the door panel slid closed, Jan poked her head inside.

"After you've changed, please check in on your wards—S41-S44. Everything you need to know about them is available on their

VDU." She hesitated a moment and rubbed her brow. "Did I forget anything? Oh yes, of course. When all four residents have fully succumbed, your penance will be considered paid."

Jan's cheery expression disappeared as the doors closed. *Seriously? You can say that with a smile on your face?* Fran shook her head and then changed into her new uniform.

Her stomach balled into a knot as she stood at the entry of the first resident's quarters. Just like Chan's, the room housed a bed, locker, and shelf with an old fashioned computer. An aged man in a wheelchair sat in the center babbling to himself. Fran rapped on the doorway before entering. "Hello?"

His babbling continued without interruption. Fran stepped around the man to the video display and waved a hand in front of the screen. To her chagrin, the screen remained dormant.

"Hmmm." She tried again with no response before spying the palm-sized device next to the unit. Mom had told Fran about gadgets that Grandma had used with her computer. She snickered as she remembered Mom calling it a mouse, and then rolled the plastic thing around until the screen came to life. She employed the plastic mouse to chase a white arrow around the screen before reaching the icon that read, "Resident Information."

Once she clicked the buttons at her fingertips, data scrolled across the screen for *Bob*. Fran smiled and turned around.

"Hello, Bob. How are you?"

Bob continued babbling, and Fran returned to the video display to read through his history. Bob had been a schoolteacher at one time. She faced Bob and scrutinized his mannerisms as he babbled. Although unable to understand the words, Fran did notice familiar gestures like those of her old teachers—a lift of a brow, nod of the head, and occasional pointing of a finger. She experienced a surreal shiver. Although his classroom ceased to exist in this world, Fran had a suspicion that somewhere in Bob's world, he continued to teach.

She watched him for a few more moments and then shrugged. He seemed content. She moved on to meet her next ward.

Room 242 belonged to John—a fact he plainly stated as soon as Fran entered. Although he seemed lucid, Fran soon discovered that on John, everything hurt. All the time. And John demanded relief. *Pronto*. She tended to a few of John's nonexistent ails before moving on with a promise to return soon.

Room 243 brought a surprise as it housed a celebrity from her childhood. Fran remembered watching Marie Morigeau perform on the main stage a decade prior. With her head resting on Mom's soft shoulder, Fran had felt as if she could float on the notes of Marie's lovely music. Now, however, the same woman hummed a continuous monotone note as she sat in her chair with unseeing eyes. Fran felt a stab of grief and moved on to the last room.

Fiona in room 244 barked out orders and kept Fran scurrying from one task to another. She insisted her room was stifling, and Fran smiled and adjusted the temperature. A moment later, however, Fiona claimed she was going to freeze to death, and demanded a blanket. She growled that her throat was closing up from thirst, and Fran rushed to get her some water. However, when she returned, Fiona slept comfortably in her chair. Fran huffed. *Must be from the West Wing*.

Given a guess, Fran estimated Marie to be the oldest of her wards, at about thirty five, and John and Bob not too far behind. Fiona's age remained more of a mystery. With a face full of makeup and her head donned with fashionable wig, she resembled a woman in her early twenties. However, the decline gnawed on the rest of her body, giving evidence that twenty had been a long time in Fiona's past.

Although Fran's quirky patients suffered from various levels of decline, they were her team. Team Fran. She pledged to stay with these four until the end… Or until she found her way out—whichever came first.

Over the next few days, Fran began to enjoy the eccentricities and banter of her team while touching their soft hands and whispering words of encouragement. It lulled her emptiness, reminded her of the hope that lay ahead. She knew it would be hard to say goodbye to every one of them. Yet, knowing where they were headed when their time came, she would celebrate a silent victory.

In between visits, Fran nosed around the corners of the Ranch hoping to find a clue as to the whereabouts of the portal to the open air. Although she now understood the tidy layout of the Ranch, the location remained a mystery.

After assuring Fiona to be comfortable, Fran slipped from her room and padded down the hallway in the papers booties referred to as proper footwear. Her back itched from the scratchy low-grade material she wore, and with a roll of her eyes wondered who in the world ever thought up the idea of making scratchy, canvas shirts. If she saw that person on the outside, she planned to give him a piece of her mind.

As she swished along the hallway, the buzz of a venting sounded, and Fran hurried to the nearest shaft just as Pete wriggled from the opening. Although not quite as combed as it had been a few days prior, his wavy hair still looked cute tucked behind his ears and his brown eyes, just as captivating. She liked Pete. As a matter of fact, maybe she even *really* liked him. Their gaze locked, and Fran lifted her chin toward a deserted room a few doors down.

She hadn't even realized how much she'd missed Pete over the last few days, until he wiggled his brows with unexpected levity.

"You're a handful, Mr. Pete," Fran laughed.

"That? Coming from the Wolf?" He stepped closer and reached for her hand. "Let's see this bad boy."

On inspection, Pete let out a low whistle. When Fran giggled, he dropped her hand and lifted his gaze. "So, did you read Chan's notes?"

"Mm hm." The smile felt good on her face.

"And?"

"*And,* I'm going to find the portal."

"Really?" Pete stepped forward and draped his long arms over her shoulders. Fran released an easy breath and didn't even push him away. In reality, she kind of wanted to close the six inch chasm and get lost in his cheap cologne.

"Mm hm. Why wait for the decline, right? But, I'm going to need some help." Fran took a baby step forward and wedged her head in the hollow beneath his chin.

"Just name it."

Fran enjoyed the vibrations of his voice. She hesitated before pulling away and holding up her wrist. "I need to get this thing off. I've been thinking about how to do that, and wondered if maybe Folsom could fashion something."

"Hmm. I'm sure he'd consider it an honor to at least try."

Fran smiled. "Thanks, Pete."

"Mm Hmm, I'll swing by his niche after I leave."

A sudden howling in the hallway interrupted their soft banter. Fran recognized Fiona's boisterous screams and the corners of her mouth took a dive.

"I have to go."

She raced out of the room as a crash sounded and a deep male voice rang out between howls. She rushed down the hallway and around the corner, almost colliding into a guard as he towered over Fiona's chair. Fiona cowered and wept as the guard shouted out insults and ridiculed her. Fran positioned her body between the two and looked up at the assailant.

She hadn't seen him since her school days, but the blood in his eyes still evoked the same response. With a rumble in her throat she snarled, "Freddie."

Behind Fran, Fiona continued to whimper. Freddie's face lit up, and he bore his teeth like an animal.

"What are you going to do, Monde? Kiss me?"

He puckered up and lunged toward Fran. When she ducked, Freddie stumbled onto Fiona's lap which made the old woman screech even louder. Freddie spit out a string of curses as he stood and then launched Fiona backwards. Fran sucked in her breath as the chair careened into the wall. Freddie laughed. Although she wanted to pummel his fat face, Fran rushed to the aid of the Fiona instead.

"He hurt me. That man hurt me," Fiona whimpered.

Fran rubbed her shoulders to help soothe the poor woman.

Then she turned back to Freddie.

"What were you thinking?"

"Oh, for crying out loud, Monde, she's halfway to death's door. I was just helping her along."

Fran harrumphed. "She's looks very alive to me."

"We'll see," he snickered. "When you've been here as long I have, you learn to see the signs. This one? I'm betting she'll be gone before the week's out." He grunted and shook his head before heading back down the hallway. "Have fun."

Fran continued to sooth Fiona, as she moved her back into the safe environment of her own room, stroking Fiona's faux head of hair and whispering words of encouragement. Finally, Fiona's chin dipped and a light snore followed.

"Don't worry, Fiona, soon you'll be heading out." The words slipped from Fran's lips a moment before her drawn brows lifted to her hairline and a strange congruency of grief and joy flooded her soul. Fiona would be heading *out* soon. It was an arrow pointing straight to the portal. She ran from the room and swished down the hallway.

"Hey, Freddie. Wait up."

Fran followed Freddie into the small break area and watched with sick fascination while he dissected his food. He tore a brown gooey sandwich, or pie, or something, into pieces and slurped on the ends. Although repulsed by his table manners, Fran decided sharing a meal might help mend fences. She retrieved her lunch from the cooler, popped the lid from a cold aluminum cup, and scooped a spoonful of applesauce into her mouth.

"So, where do they go?"

Freddie looked up. "Who?"

Fran shrugged while trying to contain her disgust. Her eyes seemed to roll on their own these days, so she lowered her lids to cover their inference.

"The post-primers. You know, when we send them off. Where do we send them to?"

Freddie snorted. "Who cares? They're just gone, that's all."

"Well, someone has to bring them to wherever they go. Don't you do that?"

"Nope. That's done by the higher-ups. The old guys." He continued dissecting and chomping.

"Superiors?"

"I guess." He shrugged. "All I have to do is swipe this little button." Freddie held up his com device, and his chest puffed out.

"Wow. Do I have one of those?"

He sputtered brown bits of food onto the table. "Sure, Monde." He shook his head. "You know, I've racked up two years in this joint. Maybe if you can make it that long, they'll give you the chance to send off a few. For now? Just be glad you're not pulling diaper duty."

Fran couldn't decide whether to be excited or sad for Fiona. Nevertheless, she stayed close to the woman's side for the next few days, and just as Freddie predicted, her health did take a dive. When Fiona barked, her orders became more and more delusional until Fran understood they no longer dwelt on the same plane of reality. Not only that, but her body began a rapid descent as well. Although Fiona held her own spoon on Tuesday, by Thursday, the food trolley stopped in her room three times a day to shovel in the porridge. Fran stood by and watched as the mechanized arm scooped globs from a tall bucket and dumped the contents into Fiona's awaiting mouth. Sometimes the gruel made it in. Sometimes it didn't. Either way, the arm kept moving.

When Friday rolled around, Fran stopped by to wake Fiona. The woman's eyes barely fluttered when Fran called out her name. She placed her face next to Fiona's. The weak stream of breath trickling from the resident's nose and mouth indicated such a vulnerable state, Fran feared if Fiona didn't get out to the open air immediately, she would expire in this tortured world.

Fran swished out of the room in search of Freddie, with a strong hunch where he might be found. Sure enough, as she raced into the break room, she found him seated at the table, catching the latest gaming match and munching on a package of cookies.

"Freddie, its Fiona."

He looked up and continued chewing. After dipping his hand back into the packet, he pulled out another cookie and then shoved it into his full gullet. He swallowed, took a slug from a large plastic thermos, released a sigh, and stood.

"Did you say your goodbyes, pretty lady?"

Fran had no intention of taking Freddie's bait. "She's ready. You can call the Superiors."

Freddie kept his eyes on Fran, lifted the com device, and, without even bothering to glance at it, swiped his finger across the screen.

"Done." He moved a little closer to Fran and licked the crumbs from his lips. "Now what?"

She backed out of the room. "I'll go check on my remaining residents."

Freddie chuckled. "One down, three to go. At this rate, you'll be rid of this stink before you know it."

Fran ignored his last comment as she hurried back to the room. For her plan to succeed, her timing needed to be impeccable.

Chapter Sixteen

As she neared Fiona's room, Fran spied a yellow-uniformed worker rolling the dying woman away. Belted into the moving chair with a porridge-stained wrap sagging on her wilted frame, Fiona seemed unaware of the move. One bony shoulder peeked out from where her smock had fallen away, and her bare feet dragged on the ground, making a sick scraping sound. Her shaved head, which had always remained hidden beneath a stylish wig, now exposed her hairless scalp and lobbed about like a heavy ball on a wobbly stick.

Fran waited for the worker to pass and after a few extra breaths, turned to follow him. Every so often, Fiona looked as if she might topple forward, before the orderly yanked on her shoulder to right her back into the chair. Fran followed at a distance holding back at each juncture and peeking around the corner before moving forward.

At the third intersection, as Fran spied around the corner, the yellow uniform halted mid-hallway, set the brakes for Fiona's chair and turned around to depart. Fran dove into a nearby room and waited until the footsteps swished away before moving around the final corner.

She neared Fiona and, with relief, noted a supply closet with a swing-style door located in her periphery. Fran swiped her employee code and wormed into the closet, using caution to leave the door ajar just a crack. As she watched, Fran fought the urge to run out and tend to the old woman, itching to straighten Fiona's smock and speak words of comfort. Before she could talk herself out of the closet, however, two men in matching red suit jackets, approached the chair.

Fran's spine straightened as she watched a red light flash from a hidden sensor. A voice announced their Superior credentials, and the wall hummed opened revealing a human guard on the other side. Outfitted with a breathing apparatus like the ones fashioned for would-be earth trekkers, the guard saluted the Superiors and handed over a mask for each of them. The Superiors adjusted their masks before pushing Fiona through the opening, out of Fran's view.

She cracked the door until she could see past the opening into a vestibule. The three stood before what looked like an elevator door which soon opened as well. A moment later they disappeared with Fiona through the second set of doors.

Fran charged out of the room and skidded to a halt at the opening of the first chamber. A warm and foreign atmosphere with a thick, damp quality emanated from the room. Fran breathed the strange air into her lungs. It tasted sweet on her tongue and made her head feel heavy. *Could it be air from the outside?* She inhaled a long breath and as she did, the panel hummed to a close, returning the wall between her and the portal.

Fran contemplated her new discovery for a fraction of a moment and then scurried away for fear the Superiors would return and find her gawking at the panel. Had she just pulled outdoor air into her lungs? If so, it hadn't sent her into choking death spasm, and as far as she could tell, her face remained intact—not even a drop of melted skin on her canvas shirt.

A smile grew on her face. She wanted to scream with joy. She couldn't wait to tell Pete.

.~.

The next day, her work shift began bright and early. After changing into the required Canvies, Fran yawned and swished down the hallway. As she passed a vent opening, she heard a "Psst."

Fran's gaze brushed past the grate just as Pete lifted an imprinted cheek from the mesh. She smiled. Good old mesh-face. She leaned down and whispered. "Meet me two hallways over at the fifth vent. I've got some new findings."

Fran hurried to meet Pete at the opening just a few yards from where the Superiors had exited with Fiona the day prior. Checking her back every few steps, she swept down the corridor, made a left and two rights before arriving breathlessly before the vent opening. A soft hum later, Pete unfolded from the dark.

She grabbed his arm, tugged him to the hidden panel, and whispered. "This is it."

With lifted brows, Pete opened his mouth to speak, but Fran quickly shushed him. Then she lifted a nervous finger to the inconspicuous sensor pad before pointing to her own eyes. She pressed her lips to Pete's ear and breathed out, "That's how the Superiors got in."

Before Pete could do or say anything stupid and alert the guard stationed on the other side of the door, Fran nudged him down the hallway while holding in her own breath. Once they turned the corner, she exhaled loudly. "Can you believe it?"

"No I can't. So how does it all work?"

"I'm still not one-hundred percent sure. However, this is where they bring the residents. I saw the Superiors wheel Fiona into that chamber before they disappeared through another door."

"Well," Pete looked at the floor and squirmed a little. "What if they're just bringing them to an incinerator or something?"

"Seriously?" Fran grabbed Pete by the shoulders. "What's wrong with you? You read what Chan said. It's the way out. Anyway, I saw them put on special breathing masks."

"Okay, okay." He took a step back. "So, how do we get in? Or, should I say, out?"

Fran chewed on her lip. "I'm not sure yet. But there's got to be a way."

"To bad we can't just climb through the vents," Pete chuckled.

"Mm-Hmm." Fran thought about the thick air she'd inhaled yesterday right before the panel had slid shut. If it had really come from outside, certainly a vent would be involved.

"Pete. You're a genius."

Pete smiled and wiggled his brows. "Oh speaking of genius, I've got something for you that might help things." He rummaged around in his front pocket until he produced a small band of metal.

"What is it?"

Pete chuckled. "Folsom calls it the deactivator-*plus*."

Fran's eyes grew wide. "I love that guy!" She grabbed the strip from Pete and turned it over in her palm. "A deactivator. Nice." She nodded in approval. "So what's the plus for?"

Pete chuckled. "It deactivates your bangle, *plus* gives security a pseudo reading every ten minutes. Your little bangle—while tucked away on a shelf somewhere—will appear to move about the Ranch, head home at the end of the day, and even come back for morning check-in..." His brows danced and he spoke from the corner of his mouth. "...In case you want to have an overnighter elsewhere."

Fran snorted. "What you mean *overnighter*?" She grabbed his arm. "What did you tell him?"

"Um... I just said you and I were..." He shrugged. "...You know."

Fran huffed. "Um, no. We're *not*." She mocked Pete's brow wiggle before rolling her eyes. "But, hey, thanks for ruining my reputation."

Pete chuckled and shoved his hands his pockets. The old stirrings of irritation prickled Fran's skin. She wrapped her arms around her waist.

"What?" He had that idiot look again.

"I don't want *whatever* it is going on between us to get around."

Pete lifted his shoulders and his brow arched to his hairline. "Too late?"

"What? Who'd you tell? What'd you say?"

Pete looked away and coughed. "Nothing really. I mean I might have mentioned what an awesome kisser you are." He dropped his voice. "To a couple of guys."

He turned back to Fran with mock sincerity and an obvious look of male triumph in his eyes.

She wanted to punch him.

Instead, she placed her hands onto her hips and glared. Her thawed heart began to re-freeze around the edges and she offered a phony smile before pushing Pete back toward the nearest vent.

"You better go now. We can't get caught this late in the game."

As she watched Pete crawl back into her old world, Fran reflected on their last kiss. No warm fuzzies. No butterflies fluttered in the stomach. Nothing other than frustration filled her gut.

Chapter Seventeen

Several days later Fran watched the trolley feed Marie, and cringed at the familiar signs of finality. Marie's nonsensical songs had died down to a soft hum over the last few days. And today? Not a solitary note. Fran saw the white flag being waved by her new, old, friend.

Another glop of porridge dripped from Marie's chin as the feeding trolley beeped indicating the end of her meal. The machine hummed as the spooning lever folded back into its metal belly, and the bucket dropped into the refueling chamber. Then, the trolley whirred away, moving on to the next hungry resident.

Fran hovered at Marie's side. Using the paper bib, she wiped the remaining cereal from the woman's delicate skin and spoke soft words of encouragement. Marie sighed, and a moment later, her chin fell onto her chest, followed by a light snore.

While Marie slept, Fran moved about the room, touching odds and ends that had accompanied the woman to the Ranch—her most cherished trinkets. Fran opened a small wooden box which housed a delicate silver bracelet. Underneath the bracelet sat a paper folded in half. Fran pulled it out. Once opened, she recognized it as an antique photograph revealing a girl, probably a little older than Fran. Her skin seemed lit with a glow, and glossy, brown hair hung past her shoulders. A light danced from the crown of her head as she looked at something outside of the picture. Judging from the girl's smile, whatever or whoever it was, must have been special. A carpet of green grass lay beneath her bare feet, and a wilted flower dangled from her fingers. She wore plain clothing—some sort of very short, blue pants with frayed edges and a sleeveless shirt. She looked simple, unpretentious, and plain, yet more beautiful than anyone Fran had met in this city. Who was this ancestor? Marie's great grandmother? Fran looked over her shoulder to the woman asleep in the bed. With her shaved head and white skin, Marie could pass for the girl's grandmother. The insidious Beast slithered through Fran's gut.

    A foul odor filled the room. *Again.* Fran cringed. Five consecutive accidents, deemed a resident unfit for life and *ready for takeoff* by Freddie's standards. And Fran suspected this odor marked Marie's fifth.

    She pulled the com device from her pocket and spoke into the screen to alert Pete that the mission was about to begin.

    "*S*3*4*." Pete would know what that meant.

Next, she rushed to the break room where Freddie munched flavored popcorn with one hand while his other hand hovered over his reader.

"Marie is ready."

Freddie looked up. "Congratulations, Monde. You're halfway there."

He slid the com out of his pocket and swiped the screen before returning his attention to his popcorn-smudged reader.

"I don't know why you're still standing there. Last time I checked, Bob and John were still alive."

Fran raced out of the break room. Down the hallway. A left and then two rights. She swiped her code and entered the closet. *Hurry up, Pete.*

She rolled up her pant leg and fished around her nylon sock to retrieve the strip of metal adhesive. She clipped it over the edges of the bangle, and a soft click later, the shackle opened. After placing the bangle on the shelf, Fran cracked the door just as the yellow-clad orderly arrived with Marie.

Where are you Pete?

The Ranch worker departed, and Fran waited. Her stomach pitched. The aroma of Freddie's popcorn seemed to flood her senses. She wanted to throw up, but focused on her mission. She replayed every element as hot adrenaline coursed through her veins.

The red suit-jackets arrived. After a flash, the wall slid open. The guard saluted the Superiors, handed over their breathing masks, and Marie's chair rolled out of sight. A moment later, Fran heard the hum of elevator and knew they were gone.

She waited a full second before racing from the closet and scanning the hallway for Pete. Where was he? Fran backed into the open vestibule and lingered in the rich aroma of fresh air until the hum of the panel captured her attention. She was down to two choices. Either exit quickly the way she'd entered, or take a chance on the vent overhead. With each nanosecond that passed, her options began to diminish.

Fran ran and leapt with outstretched arms. Her fingers sunk into the casing, the impact ripping her flesh. Her left leg scraped the vent, and metal tore through her Canvies. She hung for a fraction of a second, with two hands and a foot grasping the edge while leg number two kicked through empty air. On a growl, she yanked her dangling limb up and then rolled into the musty chute.

Mammoth fan blades stood between her the rest of the passage. It made sense. If they were pulling in air from outside they'd need to propel it forward. It also made sense that the fan would likely kick back on in a matter of seconds.

She flattened her body against the metal floor and bellied under the razor sharp blades. Just as her paper slippers cleared the space, a roar sounded through the chute and the fan began to move—gaining speed until the three blades blurred into one massive arm. Her body dripped with sweat. She turned and looked down the shaft. And saw light.

Chapter Eighteen

As she hovered in the vent, Fran considered the air which now permeated her lungs. Sure, she knew it didn't *really* house a myriad of poisons and knew her face wouldn't melt. Instead, new concerns danced around her brain, like *what's out there?* She remembered the lore of the Geiger Zombies from her childhood — how they would kidnap and feed on the flesh of Impervious children. She wished she would stop shaking. They were only fables.

Right?

On the precipice of crawling out of the shadow, with just a breath between her and the new world, a breeze touched Fran's matted curls. It soothed her head like a minty exhale, and a tingle surged from the cool sensation down to her toes. A great light enveloped her head burned her eyes. She clamped he lids and bellied the remaining few feet out of the shaft. Tears welled up under her lids and she slowly drew open her eyes. Black dots danced and swirled in her vision. Her brain felt unraveled like when she awoke from the EMP incapacitation. She paused and blinked a few times, to give her vision a moment to clear. She tried to stand on wobbly legs, but instead collapsed onto her knees and sat shaking and panting.

As her eyes adjusted to the brightness, her vision cleared. The shaking lessened. She stood and surveyed the landscape.

Shoot me in the head.

Bright green grasses rolled out like a carpet up and down soft hills, and tiny purple and yellow flowers scattered throughout the meadow like candy sprinkles on a birthday cake. Fran turned in a slow circle and held her breath. In one direction, a smoky mountain range emerged from the earth, and tall trees stood shoulder-to-shoulder creating a forest in the other. She looked up into a clear blue sky, dizzy with vertigo as her eyes continued to look higher and higher. The enormity overwhelmed her senses—as if it had no boundaries. She knelt back down to clutch the metal, closed her mouth, and wiped her tearing eyes.

Upon surveying her surroundings again, she could see she stood elevated from the ground on a narrow metal structure. She moved to the edge of the roof to assess the distance to the ground and realized it was probably only eight or ten feet. Should she jump?

As she considered her options, she heard a whimpering close by. *Marie?*

While remaining prone on the slick, warm surface, Fran inched to the edge until her head and shoulders cleared the roof. She peeked over the shelf and saw Marie on the ground in a heap, shivering and whimpering. Alone. The idiot Superiors had dumped her. Like taking out the daily trash, they had opened their doors and tossed her out. She pictured them using the heels of their shiny, Superior shoes to push her onto the grasses and out of the confines of their shimmery city. She envisioned their fancy red suit jackets and ridiculous HAZMAT breathing apparatuses. *Morons.* She almost wished they had stayed so she could jump onto their velvet backs and throttle their idiot faces.

Suddenly shouts filled the air and footsteps thumped on the soft earth. Fran inched backwards to employ Rebel invisibility skills. With one eye barely peeking over the edge, she spied the intruders.

A woman, dressed in a thigh-length white gown, knelt over Marie and tossed a side satchel onto the ground. A dark braid meandered down her back, and her skin glowed with warmth. Fran's eyes darted to the person squatting next to the woman. Boy? Man? Somewhere between the two? His smooth skin was like that of a boy, but Fran saw traces of a shadow over his lip. Wavy, golden hair brushed his shoulders, and rays from the sun haloed his head. His exposed arms and chest teemed with knotty muscles making him appear older than his face implied.

His arms and legs looked ripped like the late Gillius Thunder thighs, but unlike Gillius, he didn't seem to have a problem straightening his arms. He wore mid-shin pants fashioned from some sort of animal skin. The woman ran a hand along Marie's forehead and over her scalp. She reached into her bag and pulled out a packet of some sort which she held to Marie's lips inducing a soft moan from Marie.

"Get me the water."

The woman's voice rang out strong and clear. Her command direct. The young man released a leathery looking container which hung from his belt, and held the opening to Marie's mouth. Fran remained mesmerized by his strange coupling of strength and compassion. Then, he looked up.

Fran sucked in her breath.

His eyes flashed gold, and he whispered something to the woman. She looked up as well. Fran froze, her muscles paralyzed the way they did when a Graphie sent out a shockwave. The two continued to gawk at Fran, making her wonder which was odder. Her hanging out on the roof? Or them tending to a dying resident?

"Who are you?" The woman's unwavering voice resonated across the plain. Again, strong and direct.

"My name is Sarah Monde."

"What is your purpose? Are you from the Council?"

Fran laughed. "Not in a million years."

She noticed the young man chuckle. The woman tried to hide her smile. "Are you Accountable?"

Surprised to hear the common phrase spoken out here, Fran jerked back. She never considered the fact that the Council might be ruling out here as well. It never dawned on her there would be any political structure at all. She couldn't decide which answer would be the right one.

"I'm not. I mean I used to be, but I'm not now. Well, at this moment, I suppose I am." Her answer sounded deceptive even to her own ears.

The woman turned to the young man. "Retter, take care of her. I'm going to tend to this one."

The young man she called Retter pulled a long cord from his belt and tied a stone to the end. He lassoed it through the air a few times before releasing it over his head. The rope made a whizzing sound as it whipped up over the roof and made contact with a skinny metal bar. It coiled around the bar, spinning until it circled several times. Retter tugged on the end and smiled at Fran.

"Okay. You can climb down."

Fran crawled over to the rope and jerked it a few times. It seemed safe. Maybe. *How hard could it be?* She grabbed the rope and swung her feet over the side of the structure.

"Don't slide. The rope will burn your hands. Just gently repel off the side."

She had no idea what he meant. *Here goes nothing.* She swung her body around and held on tight to the cord. As her hands slipped just an inch down the rope, her feet careened into the metal siding with a loud crash. Her silent paper booties slid on the metal wall. She couldn't get a good grip and chided herself for looking ridiculous and clumsy.

"That's it. Just like that," Retter encouraged as she inched down. "Not too fast."

About four feet from the ground, she let go, landing first on her feet and then toppling onto her bottom. Retter came over and offered her assistance, which she ignored. Too humiliating. Instead, she rose to her feet, brushed off her bruised backside, and looked square into his strange, tawny-colored eyes. *Weird.*

The woman shouted, "Now, Retter!"

Before Fran understood the implication, Retter grabbed Fran around the waist, tossed her over his meaty shoulder, and took off running.

Chapter Nineteen

The landscape became a blur of greens and purples as Retter trotted through the high grasses. Her head hung over his shoulder as they bumped along, and blood pounded past Fran's temples, making it hard to think. She kicked and pummeled at his back, but he kept his stride long and moved at a good clip, hopping over large rocks as if he knew the exact location of each stationary object.

Two words ran in circles through her brain...

Geiger Zombie.

When they reached a line of trees, they stopped and Retter deposited Fran onto the mossy ground with a thud. She stood and scrambled backwards but collided with a tree. The sharp edges of the rough bark poked through her Canvies and jabbed into her flesh.

"Sit there," Retter mumbled, as he pulled out the same cord he had used to get her down from the roof.

Knowing she couldn't outrun him, Fran slid down to the ground. He wrapped the length of the scratchy rope around her wrists. After giving it a slight tug, apparently, satisfied with his work, he backed away.

While keeping his attention trained to Fran, he pulled a knife from a pocket attached to his pant leg. Fran gasped, and Retter looked amused as he yanked a tree limb from over his head. He stripped the thin bark with his knife and gave Fran another look of amusement before squatting low and finally settling onto the ground.

They sat without speaking for what seemed like a long time to Fran. He whittled the tree limb and as the sun relocated in the sky, shadows spread throughout the forest. Finally, he spoke.

"Why did you come out here?" His deep voice held little inflection, almost sounding bored.

"I read the diary of Doc. I wanted to see if it was real."

"Who's Doc?"

"I don't know. I never met him. Chan did."

"Who's Chan?"

"My mentor."

Retter looked up from his project. "Why did you come here?"

"I just told you…" *What does he want to hear? Maybe this was just part of the cannibalistic torture. Marinate their flesh in anger. It's delicious!*

They danced around this small circle of inquiry until her answers sounded confusing. She rolled her eyes and leaned her head back onto the hard bark.

"Just kill me already."

Retter looked Fran in the eye and raised a single brow. The corner of his mouth twitched, like he wanted to laugh but restrained himself. Their eyes remained locked and warmth rose up into her cheeks. *Embarrassed by a cannibal? I'm pathetic.*

A commotion in the woods unlocked the stare and both heads turned in the direction of the noise. As the outline of three figures moved toward them, Fran froze. *This is it. I'm toast.*

"Retter?" The familiar voice rang out. Fran recognized it as the women from earlier.

"Over here, Tanya."

A moment later, she came into view. A light wind rustled through the trees, and like when a curtain pulls back for a show, the shadow lifted. Traces of sunlight streamed into their space, illuminating her smile and the faces of her companions.

Fran sucked in her breath. Was she seeing a ghost? Her heart raced, and her head spun in dream-like shock. Time took on a slow and strange continuum — each moment reading like an entire story. Fran experienced every separate beat of her own heart as a measured pulse throbbed in her ears. Her eyes locked onto a face from the past and watched the pin-sized pupils staring back at her grow with mirrored shock. Brows climbed high onto the familiar forehead, and lids lifted to capacity. Lips that had kissed her cheek as a child made the shape of a perfect 'O' while two hands reached out to bridge the distance between them. The shriek pierced Fran's soul.

"Frannie!"

Surprise, fear, grief, joy, anger, forgiveness, and elation erupted from Fran like a fiery volcano. She opened her mouth, but no sound came forth. Emotions sailed through the air and scattered in the wind. Fran's heart exploded; she was sure of it. She drew in a ragged breath and sobbed,

"Mom."

Fran's mother struggled to reach around Retter and touch her daughter's face. "Oh Frannie, beautiful Frannie."

Tanya's voice rang out clear. "Retter, cut the ropes."

When the ropes severed, Fran sprang free and latched onto her mother. Painful spasms of grief retched from her soul, while joy beyond understanding burst through her spirit. Her body shook with emotion. Mother clung to daughter and whispered her name as Fran inhaled the essence of love that encapsulated her first fourteen years of life.

Her mother held Fran at arm's length, inspecting her child.

"Oh, Sweet Frannie, you are a sight." She laughed as she ran a hand along Fran's curls. "I just don't understand. *How* are you here? You're not even sick."

She rambled with laughter, questions, and tears, then back to laughter, obviously shaken by Fran's sudden appearance. "Did you come out alone?"

Fran gazed into liquid blue eyes which mirrored her own, and knew exactly what her mom was asking.

"Ted's married, Mom." Fran heaved a sigh. "He lives in the West Wing."

Fran's mother lifted a hand to her mouth. A miniature gasp suggested she understood the unspoken implication of living on the trendy side of town. No one lived there without somehow selling out to the Council. Her mother understood that either Ted or his wife were in cahoots with the top dogs. A trembling lip displayed fear for her son.

"Does he know the truth?" Her mother's voice was a whisper and a man—one who haunted the depths of Fran's memories—placed a leathery hand on her mother's shoulder.

He wore his sandy-brown, wavy hair shoulder length, and a sprinkling of gray strands winked in the sunlight. His jaw line, the slope of his nose, and the shape of his eyes reminded Fran of her brother. A grin lit up his face.

"Sarah Frances?"

Chapter Twenty

"Dad?"

Fran's father had declined long before she had begun to formulate any solid memories. From his wide shoulders to his coarse stubbly beard, he appeared rough and strong. Yet, eyes, like warm chocolates wrapped in crinkled paper, sparkled with laughter giving him a softer side. In spite of herself, Fran giggled and corrected her father.

"It's Fran."

"Sarah Fran?" he teased.

She bubbled again. "Just Fran."

"Well, I guess you could say I've waited *your* whole life to meet you."

He knelt down on one knee like a king welcoming home royalty. "It is my greatest pleasure, my lovely Sarah Fran." He held out his hand.

Fran lifted her own in response, and he brushed her fingers with a feathery kiss. With that one gesture, the past year of her life—with all of its dark tunnels, dirt, and hunger—vanished. She'd been transformed from a Rebel to a daughter.

Tanya smiled as she apologized to Fran for the rough treatment. "It's not that you looked particularly threatening, but we have to be cautious. The arm of the Council can be quite long."

Fran nodded a foggy agreement.

Retter walked up and clapped her on the shoulder. "If I'd known you were Ian's daughter—"

Fran shook her head. "It's okay. I get it."

He held out his hand, palm facing skyward. "Ret."

Recognizing the truce, she stretched out her hand palm facing up like his. "Fran."

The corner of Ret's mouth lifted into an almost perceptible

grin. He turned Fran's palm face down and grabbed hold of her forearm. She noticed his rope-like muscles and the warmth of his touch. As they stood with arms linked, he added, "Welcome, Fran."

"Fran are you hungry. Or thirsty?" Her mother's concern cut through the awkward silence.

"Yes," Fran laughed. "As a matter of fact, I'm dying of thirst."

Ruth unhooked the water satchel from her belt and handed the container to her daughter. "Of course you are."

Fran opened her mouth and poured in a large swig of the cool water. Her eyes shot open and she spat out the contents.

"Mom. Something's wrong with this water."

"It'll take some getting used to Sarah-Fran." Her dad chuckled at Fran's animated shock. "Don't worry; there's nothing wrong with the water. It's pure. Simple. Hasn't been tampered with."

Fran stared at the flask in her hand. *Of course* it tasted different. How could it *not*? Everything out here left a unique flavor on her lips.

Tanya nudged the group along. "Come on. Let's get back to camp."

As Tanya led the way, Fran followed with her mom on one side and her dad on the other. With so much excitement, Fran had failed to take the time to examine and appreciate this world. Now, however, as they moved through the woods, her surroundings opened up like a storybook.

An invisible respiration stirred the earth's surface and she closed her eyes to feel the breeze. As it circled her head, the air whispered a litany of words as if from a secret language. She opened her eyes to the sun glinting off a shiny rock. A moment later, the same object disappeared into a shadow. She lifted her face to the clouds and marveled as they shape-shifted across the sky. Leaves rustled, grasses swayed, and unseen creatures scurried about, leaving a wake of activity. An aroma appeared on the wave of a breeze, like sweet honey. After a quick inhale, it drifted away leaving a spicier smell, all peppery and green. Fran hardly knew what to expect from moment to moment. It was as if this world had a life of its own.

She glanced at her mother for the hundredth time as they walked, still shaken up with the impossible reunion. Mom squeezed her hand as if parroting her thoughts and Fran smiled. Tanya hopped over a fallen tree in the line of the path, and Fran watched the woman's braid rock from side to side, amazed at her dexterity and strength.

"How old is she?" Fran whispered to her mom.

Ruth wrapped an arm around Fran's shoulder and gave her a little squeeze.

"Tanya, how old are you?"

Fran cringed at her mother's direct line of questioning.

"Well, let's see. I was called a Second-Gen, born half a decade after the war, so that makes me…"

"Forty-five??" Fran blurted.

A grunt from behind indicated Ret's amusement and flush of warmth flooded Fran's cheeks. She almost apologized, but her mother calmly continued the conversation.

"Yes, that sounds about right."

Fran shook her head in amazement. "So how long does a person…?"

"*Live*?" Her mom finished for her. We're still not sure. But Ben's pretty high up there and still going strong."

Fran gasped. "You don't mean Benjamin Leiben do you?"

"Yes, that's him."

He's still alive?" Fran's excitement mounted.

"Oh very much so," her mother responded.

Fran felt dizzy with the thought of meeting this guy and tried to recall the million questions she wanted to ask him.

As they trekked, the path narrowed forcing the party of five into a single file line. Fran's paper booties began to rip from the twigs, and soon, they looked like shrapnel. Thorns poked through her thin stockings, and she winced as they pierced her flesh. She felt a tap on her shoulder and turned to find Retter positioned at her rear.

"Have a seat." He pointed to a fallen tree.

Fran narrowed her eyes, but obliged. Ret squatted and placed her raggedy, paper-bootie-covered-foot onto his knee. He pulled out a parcel of leather from his satchel, slid it underneath her heel, and wrapped her whole foot snug into the leather confines. Afterward, he yanked a vine-like undergrowth from the ground and tied it all together. Instant boot.

"That's crazy." Fran laughed.

After doing the same with her second foot, he tapped her calf. "There. That ought to hold you until camp."

Fran was humbled. Embarrassed. And delighted.

Ret nodded to the threesome now about fifty feet away. He leaned in toward Fran and whispered, "Don't want to get too far behind. When it gets dark around here, it gets really dark."

The notion of utter darkness in an unknown world had Fran dashing to catch up with the rest of the group, and the single-file journey continued until Tanya announced,

"Just past the tree-line."

They pushed past thick foliage and suddenly the forest ended revealing a small village. Fran gawked at the community of at least a dozen low-roofed structures surrounding an enormous fire. Two strong men hefted a mammoth log onto the flames while, behind them, about a half dozen others continued to chop wood and toss it into a large pile. Captivated, Fran watched the muscular bodies of bare-chested men and modestly-covered women. They each wore a white robe that stopped just shy of their knees, made from a fabric that shimmered in the firelight. Though ages and races varied, they chattered amongst themselves, laughing and even singing as they labored. Fran considered the Agora—gathering place and social hub of Impervious. Even while thousands milled about, never did this kind of life radiate from its center. Instead, its landscape sported downcast eyes as people hurried about, bumping shoulders and cursing under their breath.

"What is this place?"

Ruth turned to her daughter, her smile radiating the same warmth as the fire. "This is Naveh... Village Number One."

"Whoa" Fran's disbelief slid out on a slow breath.

Ruth bellowed a throaty laugh. "I remember experiencing a little disbelief when I first woke."

Ian turned to his daughter. "I'm sure this all seems surreal."

Fran nodded. *Surreal? More like a scene from a childhood fairytale.*

"Don't forget, Ruth, you and I started from scratch," he added. "Sarah still has vivid memories from the inside."

Tanya began to walk toward the huts. "I'll see you all later. I'm going to check on Marie."

Fran had forgotten about poor Marie. She'd like to check in on her old friend as well. But first, Doc. And then Chan.

She turned to her father. "Dad. Can you take me to Dr. Benjamin Leiben?"

"Of course. But how do you know Ben?"

Fran blew out a hard breath. "His story is what brought me out here."

"Really?

"Yes. He kept a journal." She hesitated. "Did you know he was a Superior?"

"Hmm." Ian rubbed his chin. "*Superior*, huh?"

"Don't get me wrong. He's not a bad guy. I mean, he wasn't a bad guy."

"Well, come on. Let's take a trip to old Ben's place."

A few minutes later, they arrived, and like in a dream, her storybook character came to life. And not a holographic version of a producer's character interpretation like in the movies. No, she sat face-to-face with the living, breathing, star of the show.

"It was insidious really." Ben held the mug in his hand and sipped his tea. "Marcus didn't start out like that. As a matter of fact, when the project first began, Marcus was a source of light with a desire to save."

A woman moved to the table with a fresh pot of tea. Her gaze remained on Fran as she poured.

"Don't mind me. I'm just the doctor's wife." She winked at

Fran and turned to her husband. "Would you like some honey, dear?"

"Yes. Thank you, Ema."

Fran's head whipped around as the woman moved to a set of cupboards.

"You?"

Ema turned and smiled. "Yes dear?"

"You're alive?"

Ema laughed. "Well, I certainly hope so."

"But..."

Fran remembered Ema to be from the second generation underground. Her dark hair, braided and coiled into a bun sat at the nape of her neck, and delicate gray strands lined her temples. Deep set, brown eyes spoke of an Asian heritage and knotty muscles in her shoulders and arms reminded Fran of Retter. Ema smiled and a host of small lines accented her eyes.

"We had this planned for a long time. You should tell her how this all began, Dear."

Fran turned back to Ben as he scratched his stubbly chin. "Well, I met Marcus at MIT... more specifically at O'Malley's Pub—a popular hangout for the college crowd. We were an unlikely pairing—a trendy business major and a nerdy physics geek. Two guys who wanted to explore the 'what-if's' in life."

The years seemed to melt from Ben's face as he revisited his early days of freedom and fascination. He retold the story of two young men who shared an eagerness to put skin onto ideas that seemed centuries ahead of their time. He lit up as he recalled the ingenuity of his old friend and how they had traveled the world, drumming up financial support for a project deemed an illogical fantasy by so many.

"But then came a shift in the political climate. Small wars broke out around the globe. Terrorist activity escalated to new heights. Governments crumbled, and panic rose with strategic missiles held at the ready. That's about when bids for a shot at survival began to trickle in. Before long, the trickle became a river and the river a series of rapids. There was limited space, of course:

One thousand luxury underground condos."

Ben sighed. "Only the wealthiest were allowed in. How else could we decide? The price of a ticket eventually sold for more than several generations of wealth. You know, I guess I assumed there were only a handful of the mega-rich, but I found out otherwise."

He continued with the tale, remembering the shift in Marcus who deemed himself ruler of this elite crowd. He shared until coming to the place in the story that overlapped his diaries. But the darkest and most horrible of all questions had still not been answered. She had to know.

"What about the decline?"

Ben released a heavy sigh. "A water supply riddled with a myriad of tasteless, odorless assassins." A wisp of steam rose from Ben's mug, curled through the air, and dissolved into the vast land of the invisible.

Fran thought of Marie and Fiona's suffering and how she sat by and watched as they weakened and decayed, knowing she couldn't ease their pain. Her heart broke as she considered her mother, father, and Chan. And the hundreds—maybe even tens of hundreds—who suffered this way.

"What about the antidote?"

He shook his head. "No such thing. Just a different water source."

"But how then? How did you..." she turned to her father, "and you..." she waved her hands around the room, "and everyone else beat this poison?"

"Ah yes. My Ema is a genius." Ben's boyish grin stretched across the room even while Ema tsk'd, waving off his accolades.

"No need for humility, dear, you've put together an amazing system of detoxification and restoration." Ben tapped his eyes. "Eyesight is as good as ever."

Fran sucked in her breath and put a hand to her mouth. She had all but forgotten about Ben's blindness. Now, on closer inspection, she noticed subtle patches of skin around his eyes different than the rest of his complexion. Tight and shiny, the skin meandered out toward his temple.

"How did it happen?" she whispered.

"They injected my optic nerves with a paralytic." His laugh came out in a cynical growl.

"But?"

"But Ema, my dear, is a healer."

Ema nodded her head and joined in. "It took time, though. As you can see, some of the treatments were pretty harsh on his skin."

"But it worked?"

"I've employed the aid of some very helpful teas and herbs." She placed her index finger onto her lips and gazed into the open space. "Oh and *Curcuma Longa*, the healing plant. Definitely a very important component in the process."

Ema's precise manner of speech was that of academia and Fran considered Ema's history a moment before turning back to Ben.

"Dr. Leiben, do you remember Chan? He worked as your scribe, I think."

"Chan? Of course." Ben's face lit up. "You don't know how relieved I was to hear he was finally released. How do you know Chan?"

"He was my mentor. He saved my life."

"Yep. Sounds, about right. I'm looking forward to his final healing. He and I have a lot of catching up to do."

Fran turned to Ema. "Can I see him?"

"Of course. Come, dear."

Fran hesitated. She still had a million questions for Doc but he waved her off. "Go visit your mentor. You and I will have plenty of time for discussions."

Fran nodded, eager to see her old mentor and followed Ema across the central hearth to another structure on the far side of the fire. A line of beds rested along the far wall. Marie lay in the first bed. Tanya sat nearby, stroking Marie's hair and helping her take small sips of water.

Fran drew near to the bed. "Hi, Marie."

Marie nodded before her eyelids drooped.

"I've given her a sedative tea. The release can cause quite a shock to their system, and it allows their bodies the opportunity to begin to heal."

Fran nodded, reached into her pocket, where she had placed the folded photo and delicate bracelet. She laid them onto the low table next to Marie's bed before scanning the room. Then she saw him.

On admission to the Ranch, Chan's signature black pony had been snipped. Nubby outgrowth capped his skull, but she'd recognize his eyes anywhere—black as night, brimming with wisdom. He sat with his back against a pillow, sipping a steamy mug of tea. Fran's chest tightened as she approached his bed. Did she see a glimmer of recognition?

Ema's warning rang through her ears. *Don't expect too much change, dear. He hasn't yet fully healed.*

She rested a hip on the edge of his bed. "Hello, Chan."

He nodded and, with a shaky hand, set his tea onto the side table. He stared into Fran's face. His brows furrowed deep with concentration. She silently begged for recognition, longing for her old mentor back. The corners of his mouth dipped into a frown, and on an exasperated breath he closed his eyes. Fran waited for them to reopen, but a moment later, a light snore emitted from his mouth.

She sat and watched him sleep for few breaths, then swiped at the tear trailing her cheek and moved back to the doorway.

"Go ahead, dear." Ema hovered at Marie's bedside. "I'll be along in a moment."

Fran moved out of the hut and stood by the door. The sky had changed from soft pinks and purples to an inky black. The air felt chillier, and she shivered. Gazing up at the darkened sky, the unknown haunted her. *Would he ever be right again?*

"Sarah-Fran."

She whipped around, unaccustomed to hearing her name called out, and saw a figure from the other side of the fire. She waved her father approached.

"How is your mentor?"

Fran shrugged. "He'll probably be fine." A rush of emotions threatened to spill. "That's what Ema says."

"Mmm. I've seen dozens of healings. It's a miracle really." Fran looked up at her father and failed an attempted smile. He chuckled and rested an arm on her shoulder. "He's going to be good as new. Really."

Fran stiffened under his embrace, embarrassed by his show of affection. Then again, his strong hold felt safe. Protection. The notion melted her awkwardness a little, and she lifted her gaze to her father.

"Thanks."

He smiled down at Fran. "You bet. Listen, I know you must be exhausted, but would you like to take a little side trip before we turn in?"

"Sure. Where to?"

"Come on. I'll show you." Ian led Fran outside of the reaches of the fire and into the forest. At first, the darkness seemed as blinding as crawling through the air vents, but as her eyes adjusted, the night unfolded around her. Varying degrees of grays and blacks took shape, and soon Fran noticed bits of light filtering in between the shadowy limbs of the trees.

"Watch your step, Sarah."

Ian took hold of Fran's hand and assisted her over a hidden log. They continued to trek at a slow, careful pace and now that she was moving, she enjoyed the cool, damp air. Night smelled different than earlier in the day. Muskier. Richer. Because the animals' daytime melodies quieted to a sleepy nighttime hush, her rustling footsteps—as well as those of her father's—sounded loud, intrusive even, as they walked amid the slumbering forest.

Soon, they made their way to a border where the trees gave way to a meandering river. The waters lapped at the muddy shore and sparkled as they mirrored luminescence from above. Fran lifted her gaze skyward to the spherical moon, which looked like the head of a bald man smiling down on them. She shuddered at its eerie resemblance to the residents at the Ranch and quickly turned back to her father.

Diamonds sparkled from his eyes, and a glimmer danced upon his head as the river winked in the background. The twinkling of a few faraway stars drew her back to the inky sky. The longer she focused on the heavens, the more glowing orbs grew in abundance before her very eyes.

She smiled at her father. "Amazing."

Ian lifted his own gaze to the sky and paused as if also stupefied by the vast expanse.

"Even the intelligent creators of Impervious could not duplicate this beauty. Think about it. Such small lights. Yet, they light our path as if it's daylight."

They sat in silence, and Fran allowed herself to be spellbound by the trippy night sky until Ian sighed and gave her shoulder a protective squeeze.

"Hardly a death sentence, huh?"

"Yep. That's for sure." Fran agreed. "Hey, Dad—"

She paused. The name still sounded odd coming from her mouth, yet the title slipped out with ease. She looked up at Ian and said it again.

"Dad?"

Ian smiled, and his nostrils flared. "Yes, Sara-Fran?"

"Why hasn't anyone gone back to Impervious and told them? I mean, you know, that the earth is safe."

"Yes." He quieted and looked to the sky as if seeking an answer. "You're not the first to pose that question. But it's not that simple."

Fran waited as her father contemplated the night. "Suffice it to say, there are many safeguards in place to discourage that very thing."

Fran nodded her head, remembering the well-guarded vestibule. "I can get around the guard, you know."

Ian turned to his daughter. "I wouldn't attempt that, Sara-Fran." He shook his head to emphasize the point, as if he already knew his daughter's strong will. "Tell you what, why don't you ask

Ema about her ray scars."

"Ray scars?" Fran cringed and touched her bare arm.

"Yes. A deathly device carried by the guard protecting the portal. A shot in any major organ would render death. Fortunately for Ema, she only suffered minor damage when trying to return."

Ian continued. "Anyway, Impervieites seem happy with life the way it is. They eat, drink, and live an easy, synthetic world. Quite different than out here, wouldn't you agree?"

"I guess."

"You could say that *most* folks aren't searching for a way out." Ian shook his head. "You know, I sometimes wonder if the majority wouldn't just prefer to stay in the city anyway."

Like Ted?

Fran drew in a breath and held it tight before allowing it to seep from her lips. Surely, some of them would want to know.

They had to tell them. People needed to know that the Epoch was real. They needed to be told to stop selling out their lives for a little fame and fortune. As her father had just pointed out from the night sky, a little light could go a long way.

Chapter Twenty One

    The following day Fran lingered around the fire crew and admired the rhythm of the workers. The hypnotic thump of the axe and scream of the wood as the blade tore through the center continued for several minutes before one of the workers smiled and handed over his axe. Fran, who had been itching to give it a try, stepped up to the log and stretched her arms high overhead. She swung the sharp tool through the air, but upon impact, the hatchet simply bounced off the awaiting log.

    The man, who looked old enough to be her father, chuckled and took back his tool. As he bore down, muscles rippled through his back and his blade tore through the log. With the two halves still rocking, he turned and smiled at Fran.

    "And that's the way it's done."

    He extended his arm, palm facing the sky. "Edam." Fran grabbed his forearm and returned the greeting. "Fran. Impressive work, Edam."

    "Yeah. Not bad for an old guy."

    "Gen Three?" Fran inquired.

    Edam nodded. "Good guess."

    "Do you have any family on the inside?"

    "Of course," He answered. "A son and a wife. That's why I haven't moved on. I'll stick around until my family's complete."

    "Hmm." Fran wasn't sure how to respond.

Edam smiled. "No worries. I know I'll see them soon."

He lifted his axe overhead for another swing and Fran smiled. "Nice to meet you, Edam."

She moved away from the circle of workers toward the healing hut. Maybe today Chan would be more lucid. When she arrived, however, she found the occupants of the all the beds to be sleeping. She moved to the first bed and smiled down at Marie. Maybe one day soon, she could rest her head on mom's shoulder and listen to her sing again. As she moved past the second bed, she saw Fiona. She'd been so excited last night, she'd completely missed her first ward to be released. Fiona also dozed — mouth open and a snore gurgling through her throat. Fran wondered how this world would stack up for someone like Fiona and snickered at what lie ahead.

She passed a few empty cots before she reached Chan. She rested a hip onto his bed and sat for a moment silently wishing for him to wake. As she watched and waited, new questions swirled around her head. Would he be glad to see her? What if he was mad at her for coming out all alone? Chan snorted and Fran jumped, thinking he was waking. However, when he settled deeper into his small cocoon, she realized he was down for the count, and therefore, returned to parents' structure.

Mom jumped up when Fran entered. "Oh I'm so glad you're back. There's something I want to show you."

Fran followed her down a short path through the woods to a small opening and a spring of clear water.

"The most amazing bathtub around," Ruth announced with outstretched arms. Along the bank grew clusters of plants with long stalks covered in tiny bluish-white flowers. Ruth knelt down and yanked an entire plant from the ground.

"I guarantee you've never experienced a bath like this." She pulled a bulbous root from the clump, tossed aside a handful of tiny flowers, and handed Fran the bulb.

"All you need to do is squeeze this into your palm and, ta-dah. Instant soap."

"Mom." Fran stared at the bulb. "How in the world would someone know that?"

Ruth chuckled at her daughter's reaction. "Oh, sweetie, this is only the tip of the iceberg. Ema has taught me some amazing aspects of this natural earth. We really want for nothing." She smiled at her daughter and nodded toward the spring. "Give it a try."

The water looked clear and inviting. Large, red boulders surrounded one side of the spring, affording some privacy, but the idea of disrobing and bathing in the broad daylight? Out in the open? Not in a million years.

"Mom, what if someone comes by?"

"Oh, they won't. This the female bathing area. We each take turns and but I'm giving you my personally-allotted time. The spring and its privacy are all yours. Go ahead. Take your time. I'll fetch you a clothing for drying and some clean clothes."

Ruth departed, leaving Fran alone with the bulbous root and the clear spring. She ran fingers through her tangled curls, feeling the salty remnants of the prior day and the grit on her face as she swept a hand across her forehead.

She sniffed the flower-bulb in her hand. It smelled sweet and soapy. What the heck?

After slipping out of her Canvies, she eased into the warm, swirling waters, lowering herself until only her head remained above the surface. She moved her arms and legs in slow circles, feeling weightless as the bubbly spring waters danced across her skin.

She lifted the soap root out from below the water and squeezed its sponginess. A foamy, flowery essence trickled out. Fran giggled as she sprinkled it on her hair. The more she scrubbed, the sudsier she got. She washed her face before diving under to rinse and then cleaned between her toes and behind her ears, not wanting even a speck from the underground city to remain on her body.

Once she finished washing, she lingered in the water, gliding from one edge of the spring to the other, feeling graceful and free. She breathed in the fresh morning air and hummed along with the birds as they sang in nearby trees. Lifting her face to the sky, she enjoyed the various spotty colors floating across her closed lids.

After a luxurious soak, she noticed crinkly skin on her fingers and took it as a sign to open the spring to another bather. With reluctance, she swam to the shore where a folded soft blanket and shimmery robe awaited. She dried, tossed the robe-like dress over her head, and looked down to appreciate the dance of the sun on the fabric. A few drops of water dripped from her curls as she walked the path feeling alive and invigorated, in harmony with the dynamic world around her.

Back at the camp, Mom gave her a steamy mug of tea. It tasted bitter at first but left a sweet licorice aftertaste in her mouth. Golden warmth enveloped her body as they moved to sit by the fire.

Fran looked sideways at Mom before sipping her tea and gazing back into the fire.

"This really is amazing, Mom." They giggled together like a couple of old friends until Ruth excused herself and Fran was left alone with her thoughts. Out here in this strange new world, her underground memories seemed blurry and frightening, as if it had all been a horrible nightmare. And even though she'd known nothing else for her entire life, today it seemed preposterous to think people lived down there. Being poisoned. Walking to their death.

She thought about her brother. Had he really given in to the Impervious way? And what about Pete? Would he try to exit the portal on his own the way she had? The thought seeing Pete sent a ripple of excitement through her core. She missed his goofiness and laughed out loud as she pictured Retter running through the prairie with Pete over his shoulder.

Later in the day, she accompanied Tanya on a short scouting mission. As they took a moment to rest under the shade of an oak, Tanya inquired if Fran wanted something to eat. Like always, her mouth began to water. Tanya produced a large red sphere from her bag and held it up to Fran.

"Apple?"

"Apple?" Fran parroted. The only apple Fran had tasted had come from a can with SECURED stamped on the side. Fran squinted. "Is it safe?"

Tanya slid a knife from a sheath by her waistband. Fran took a quick step back, as Tanya smiled and held up the apple. "How about we share it?"

She cut into the fruit, and a fine spray of juice shot into the air, making Fran flinch a second time. Tanya smiled as she wiped her sticky hand.

"Go ahead. Have a taste."

Fran turned the fruit over in her hands and held it to her nose. She sniffed the flesh. The ripe aroma compelled her to move it to her mouth. On a loud crunch, she clamped down and pierced the crisp red. Another spray of nectar shot through the air, and Fran's eyes widened as the sweetmeat tickled her taste buds. Without even swallowing her first bite, she dove into the apple for more—like the french fries all over again. But better.

While munching, she kept an eye on Tanya, who seemed amused. Fran realized she had juice dripping off her chin and self-consciously swiped her face with the back of her hand.

A rustling through the woods caught their attention, and Tanya spotted a brown bear about a hundred feet away. Tanya appeared calm, and whispered a warning for Fran to remain silent and glued to the tree. With wide eyes and a pounding heart, she complied. Eventually, the bear wandered off, leaving Fran with shaky legs and a very cool memory.

Hours later, Fran strolled with her father from the central warming fire back to their cabin in quasi-silence, exhausted and relaxed at the same time. Even so, Chan's recovery nibbled at the edges of her brain.

"Dad, I'm going to visit Chan another time before I turn in. Tell mom, I'll be there in a few minutes."

She approached the darkened hut and hesitated at the doorway unsure if she should enter. Edged in the glow of the central hearth, Fran could see shadowy outlines of the beds.

"Wolf." His deep voice seemed to growl from the shadows.

Fran jumped and her heart stopped. "Chan?" His name came out on a whisper. She raced across the room to his bed. "Chan?" His name rolled from the depths of a sob.

A glow—*the moon? The fire?*—reflected from his eyes. Life twinkled from his iris and Fran could have sworn his mouth curled into a smile.

"Wolf. Go back."

"I know, I know, Chan. We have to tell them. We have to help them, right?" A tear coursed along her cheek and Fran slurped back her saliva. "Oh Chan, I've missed you so much. It's getting worse down there. I mean…"

"Chan?"

A light snore sounded.

"Chan?"

The room darkened as a cloud moved across the bright moon, and she knew Chan was out again. Fran exhaled a small sob and then pulled the covering up under her mentor's chin.

Soon he'd be back.

And she planned to make him proud.

Chapter Twenty Two

Fran lay on the comfy padding listening to the soft breath of her mom, punctuated every few minutes with a snort from her father's side of the bed. Light had just begun to filter through the trees, a prelude to the new day. Feeling rested, Fran tiptoed through the cabin, changed back into her discarded Canvies, and meandered out to the warming fire, now a pile of ash and white coals from the previous night.

She grabbed a fallen limb from a nearby tree and stirred the embers. Smoke rose from the ash, and a soft glow emanated from below the white. She reached for a few twigs, and tossed them into the pit. Soon, tiny flames frolicked around the edges. A few more twigs, and the flames began to grow.

The very same thoughts that had kept her awake most of the night swirled around her head. She knew she could get back in.

But what if I can't get back out? What if I become trapped back inside that madhouse?

She stirred the fire again and added more wood. Soon, the flames danced higher and Fran felt satisfied with her accomplishment. As the warmth lifted to her face, her new conviction overwhelmed her senses.

Just like this fire, Fran knew the flames of hope which had been doused by the Council still smoldered somewhere underground. Could lighting the way be as simple as stirring the embers? Her heart awoke with a battle-cry — a poetic response to a painful decision.

"They teach you that in the city?" Ret walked up to the fire and sat on a log next to Fran.

Fran stared into the fire, shaking her head. "No. It just kind of happened."

"Hm. Well, nice job."

She turned to face his golden eyes. "How long have you lived out here?"

He held her gaze. "Always."

"Seriously?"

Ret nodded his head. "I guess you could call me a First Gen."

Fran laughed. "I doubt that. First Gen's are like fifty years old or something."

Ret nodded. "Right. First Gen's from the city. I'm an open-air First Gen."

"Oh, I get it." Fran felt kind of stupid that she'd missed the joke. "So, how old are you, then?"

"Hmm. Good question." Ret looked up at the sky. "Probably somewhere around your age."

His grin reached across the fire, adding another layer of warmth to Fran's skin. She noticed the birds had begun their morning chatter and looked around for signs of life within the village. The camp remained quiet, but before long, bodies would wander about and join the life that had already woken. Ret poked at the fire, encouraging the flames to jump a little higher.

"Hey, Ret, can I ask you for a favor?"

He looked up. "What do you need?"

"Can you show me how to get back to where we first met?" She held her breath.

Ret stopped poking the fire, tossed the twig into the pit, and stood.

"Why not?"

She smiled and stood as well.

Ret looked down at her feet.

"Hang on." He disappeared for a minute and returned carrying a pair of suede booties. "These ought to make the journey a little easier."

Fran laced up the booties and followed a few steps behind Ret in quasi-silence. Although she respected the fact that he hadn't barraged her with a million questions about the city, the quiet soon began to feel a little awkward, even to her.

"So, Ret, how do you know your way around so well?"

Ret turned and shrugged. "It's easy."

He stopped and waited for Fran to catch up and then sidled right next to her. She could smell the outdoors on his skin and her stomach lurched as he put a hand on her shoulder. He leaned his head in close and his hair smelled like the spicy woodlands.

"See that boulder?" He pointed off into the distance.

Fran swallowed hard. "Yes."

He pulled away from her and smiled. "That marks the trail I take to the river."

He narrowed his eyes and peered through an opening to their left.

"And if you look real close, you'll find the sun has just climbed over the edge of that lowest mountain ridge."

Fran squinted to try and see what he saw. She really couldn't see it, but nodded anyway.

"That tells me where East is. I know the village sits southwest of the mountain line and just north of the river."

"Hm. Interesting. That's pretty much how I navigate the city. Except my mountain line was a moving stairway, and my village was the Agora."

They continued comparing notes as they traversed and by the time they neared the edge of the woods, critters scurried past their feet, birds fluttered and chirped, and insects hummed about their heads. When the trees gave way to fields, she sucked in her breath at the landscape of the city in the distance. A long, narrow roof, the one where Fran had stood only two days prior, rose up from the earth and meandered for a good distance before sloping back down. Cylindrical towers sat in rows, their gaping jaws taking turns spouting white smoke into the blue sky. Other than the brown grasses surrounding the perimeter, the rest of the city remained hidden and indiscernible.

Could thousands of people live below their feet, eating, drinking, and carrying on as if no other life existed but their own? The thought seemed preposterous now that she saw it from a different angle. A strange claustrophobia shook her body, and hundreds of prickly needles moved over her skin.

The earth seemed to growl, the trembling reverberations wandered up her legs. She turned to Retter.

"Do you feel that?"

"Mm hm. We call it the cries from below."

Fran shivered and wondered if she had the fortitude to go back there.

"I need to get up on the roof."

His eyes narrowed. Fran placed her hands on her hips. "Let's just say I forgot something inside."

Ret his eyes trained to the ground while Fran held her breath unsure if he planned to help her or rat her out.

Chapter Twenty Three

Fran placed a trembling hand upon the rope.

"Thank you, Ret."

Knowing if she didn't move fast, she'd risk losing her nerve, Fran scaled the rope, tossed the end back to Ret, and scurried to the mouth of the air vent. After lowering herself into the darkness, she crawled toward the roaring fan and waited for the eventual stop. As she lingered, fear consumed her thoughts and heading back to the village entered her mind more than once. But Chan's voice echoed through her mind. *"Wolf. Go back."*

When the blades halted, she bellied underneath the sharp edges and then remained concealed within the darkness only a few feet from the final opening. How long would she have to wait? She chewed on her nails until the ends bled and revisited her plan at least a hundred times in her mind.

.~.

A hum preceded the sounds of their voices. Fran held her breath as muffled conversations accented by the creaking of wheels and pulleys marked the countdown.

She snaked to the edge of the vent, and the instant the doors to the elevator closed, she sprang from the shaft. She moved breathlessly across the hallway where her bangle still hid on the shelf in the closet. With a surreal realization that nothing had changed while she was away, she clicked the bangle back onto her wrist. As she reached for the door, Fran caught a glimpse of her feet.

"Oops."

She untied Ret's booties, stuffed them back behind the shelving, grabbed a new pair of paper gems, and swished down the hallway.

She went to Bob's room first. He sat in his chair, talking to the invisible classroom. He should be good for a few hours.

She moved on to John's room. As soon as she crossed the threshold, he shared with her the story of how he stubbed his toe the week before. Since he hadn't been out of his chair since she had known him, she figured he had made the story up but still brought John a cooling pack for his toe before she left.

Fran deactivated her bangle, exited the Ranch and made a quick stop to her favorite pawn shop before hurrying back to the OE.

Employing razor-sharp incisors, Fran ripped the plastic seals off the new and trendy, DataJump, palm-readers, as she rushed into her allocated residence. The charge indicator progressed, one blue dot at a time, as the wireless amps booted up.

Fran wiped sweaty palms onto her Canvies and held the first DataJump over her reader. With a simple flick of her wrist and a brush of an icon, pages of testimony from Dr. Benjamin Leiben began to scroll first on her reader then, a moment later, onto the DataJump as well.

One down.

While the remaining DJ's loaded, Fran traded her soiled trousers for the gray miniskirt from Holding and a hooded t-shirt. Then, she tucked the three new DJ's into separate compartments of her pocket-boots, and with a quick fluff of her hair and a swipe of gloss, she headed back out to the hub of the city.

She passed a few women in shimmering metallic dresses along the way. One even boasted iridescent stockings that lit with each footstep. Fran shook her head. Eastsiders mimicking the elite? She didn't know whether to laugh or cry for these people and their ridiculous costumes. Then again, not everyone dressed weird. Some folks dressed like Fran, opting for a cheap pair of Canvies or skin-hugging Lycra. As she waited for the elevator, Fran peeked at the imitation leather pockets-boots she wore and shrugged off her own moment of fashion conviction.

Once down the elevator, and on the periphery of the Agora, a kiosk advertising markdowns on select electronics caught Fran's eye. She wanted to purchase a few more DataJumps but also wondered how many she could accrue before her purchases raised suspicion with Account Analyzers. Then again, she felt a responsibility to her Rebel brothers.

Getting the message to the well-outfitted, Accountable crowd would be far easier as it would only take a wave of the hand. After all, everyone owned a DJ… *if* Accountable. But the Unaccountable? Not so much.

After deciding upon a half dozen DJ's Fran moved toward her and Pete's old meeting spot, hoping he'd show up at some point. As she approached, her steps slowed.

What?

She slid in next to him on the bench and caught a whiff of freshly-laundered canvies. Pete turned an expressionless face her way.

"Where have you been?" His rigid jaw barely moved as he spoke.

Neatly trimmed bangs swept Pete's brow, and a crisp, upturned collar brushed the sides of his neck. Her gaze dove to Pete's wrist and she winced upon seeing the bangle.

Fran opened her mouth to speak, but nothing came out. Pete scratched at the skin under his bangle while avoiding her shocked expression. After a moment of silence, he continued.

"I went to the Ranch. Just like we planned." He looked at Fran with contempt. Did he hold her responsible for this?

"Freddie found me."

Fran found her voice. "What did you tell him?"

"Nothing. I didn't have time before they hauled me off."

"Oh, man, Pete." Fran shook her head. "When's your hearing?"

"Tomorrow." He stared at the floor.

"What about a deactivator? Can't Folsom make you one?"

Pete snickered. "Sure. As soon as I see him, I'll make sure to ask."

Of course. Fran bit her lip. House arrest meant he couldn't get into the vents. And because she hadn't been around... Why did everything have to be so hard?

She was about to offer make the trip for him but another idea entered her brain. She smiled wickedly.

"Care to join me in some Community Service at the Ranch?"

Pete lifted a brow.

"I got out, Pete."

"What? It's real?"

Fran laughed. "It's as real as the nose on my face." She lifted her brows and tapped the tip of her nose. "Chan asked me to spread the word."

Pete's mouth hung open. "You're messing with me."

"Nope." Fran crossed her arms and leaned back against the wall.

"What was it like? No zombies, right? Is Chan okay? Come on, Wolf, don't leave me hanging. What the heck?" He got all fidgety, and it brought Fran some relief to see the old Pete make an appearance.

"It's hard to explain. You're just going to have to see if for yourself." She hesitated to draw out the suspense. "How about tomorrow after your sentencing we leave together?"

Pete stood. "How about now?"

Fran shook her head. "Not yet." She tapped the bangle on his wrist. "Tomorrow, you can get there legit. And for now," she handed a DJ to Pete. "We have a mission to accomplish."

"A DataJump?"

"Not just any DJ, but rather a DJ loaded with Doc's truth. We'll use the next twenty-four hours to spread the word." She stood. "I'll take the East Court, and you can Jump the West."

As she walked away, Fran checked her shoulder. Pete remained on the bench, rolling the Data Jump in his palm.

"Tomorrow, Pete. I promise," she shouted before being caught up in the human river which she rode to the East Court.

Before long Fran hovered by a café table where a reader sat unattended—the owner a step away listening to a Graphie pitch a sale. Fran reached down as if adjusting her boot and slid the DJ from its confines. She swiped the 'jump' icon and watched pages of testimony scroll on her hand-held screen. The nearby, abandoned reader hummed to life as Doc's and Chan's testimonies launched from her DJ to the nearby drive.

Her hand shook as she waited.

Once completed, she swiped 'finish' on her device and moseyed off. After a few solid hours meandering through the Agora, jumping Doc's diary onto reader after reader, she plopped down on a nearby bench and slid the DJ back into her boot. A satisfied smile inched across her face. *Now, off to Ted's place.*

.~.

Fran stepped off the lift feeling a little queasy. This visit marked her first-ever encounter with the West Wing. From *outside* of the venting confines, anyway. The trendy, decked-out hallway boasted a colorful arc of light moving right along with Fran and gentle sounds of the ocean surf filled her ears. Once she turned a corner to a new hallway, however the ocean morphed into the soft chirping of birds. Opulent flower arrangements, straight from the greenhouse, added an ambiance of sweet rose and honeysuckle. Along the walls, inlaid video display units boasted Council messages and advertisements for trendy home décor.

Fran was certain the authorities monitored every move she made as she traversed this side of town. She would need a sneaky game plan—a way to send Ted the message—and considered her options as she walked.

When she stood before unit 624, the flat metallic doorway allowed Fran a distorted view of her own reflection. How apropos. Distorted—pretty much summed up how she felt. A moment later, she heard the announcement.

"You have a visitor."

Seriously? She waited a few moments. The door greeter chimed again.

"Ted and Nissa Monde, 624, you have a visitor."

She thought back to her old pod with its single-tone door chime and snorted as the greeter spoke again.

"Ted and Nissa Monde, 624, your presence is requested at the portal for a visitor."

Fran rolled her eyes, but a moment later, they opened wide with surprise as the mirrored door morphed into a video display. Ted's sleepy face replaced her image.

"Wickworm?"

"Hey bro." Her voice sounded raspy. Was she nervous to see him?

A moment later, the door whooshed open to a shirtless Ted wearing a silky pair of sleeping trousers.

"Come in."

Fran moved into the same living area she had peeked into from the confines of the air vent just a few days before, and her head turned to the meshed opening. Weird.

"Nice place."

"Coffee?"

Ted moved over to the kitchenette area, grabbed an acrylic mug from the shelf, and waved a hand over a shiny appliance. A moment later, the aroma of roasted beans infiltrated her senses, and a steamy cup of coffee sat at the ready. Ted repeated the action before carrying both mugs to the table.

"You look good." He smiled at his sister and lifted his mug in a mock salute. After a searing sip, he set the mug back down, and chuckled. "I'm glad you're back on the grid."

Fran nodded. *How am I going to do this?*

She knew the Council kept its finger on the pulse of every pod, and as the icy digits of security reached out and brushed against her neck, she chewed the inside of her cheek. If she could get Ted to bring out his reader, she could try to jump the diary onto it without removing the DataJump from her pocket.

"So it appears Monde Cyber Getaways is doing quite well." Fran held out her hands to indicate the luxurious pod. "What's the latest and greatest?"

Ted's chest puffed, and he sat a little taller. "I've been working on recreating Rome actually."

Fran nodded again. "Cool. I bet a lot of people will want to go there."

"Yep. The trip of a lifetime." His haughty tone and cockeyed grin felt unfamiliar to Fran. Was he now their puppet? Were the dirty fingers of the Council already manipulating his strings?

"Can I see?"

Ted's brows dipped. His head tilted. "I don't think you can be trusted."

Chapter Twenty Four

She knew Ted was only joking, but his words resonated with a deeper truth. Was anyone in this buried city trustworthy? Before Fran could respond, Nissa strolled into the room, cloaked in flowing silk.

"Mmm, I smell coffee." She spied Fran. "Oh hey, Wickerbug. Back on the grid?"

Fran's blood boiled. "I need to go now."

She walked to portico and waited for the door. Ted followed. Fran gave him a hug and whispered in his ear, "Meet me at The Waltonian at 1700."

The door breezed open, and she turned to Nissa. "And by the way, it's Wick*worm*."

Fran moved down the hallway with the greeter in her wake, "Thank you for visiting Ted and Nissa Monde. Have an enjoyable day."

She hurried off to the Ranch, and after checking on John and Bob, Fran spent the remainder of her afternoon jumping Doc's diary to the unsuspecting until her grumbling stomach reminded her that it had been several hours since her morning calzone. Fran moved to the long lunch line behind a pair of freshly-inked, gossiping femmes.

Their snug, silky frocks demonstrated the beginnings of basement-belly — a newly coined-term indicating too many lattes at the Agora. Small lights twinkled as they tapped fashionable toes.

"I heard Jean-Claude's reader was hacked." The first femme's sing-song voice and gleam implied that Jean-Claude's misery brought her a slice of joy.

The second femme rolled heavily lined eyes. "I'm sure a Rebel is at fault. Don't they have anything better to do with their pathetic lives?"

"You think?" The first clucked her tongue in disapproval. "Apparently, they deposited a story onto the hard drive. Some crazy tale of a Superior gone rogue."

"I'm sure it's just a cover for a virus. Poor guy. His whole system will probably crash in a day."

Conflicting feelings surging through Fran's veins warmed her cheeks. On one hand, the message had provoked chatter. On the other hand, were they rejecting the truth? Maybe, once they realized no virus had been attached to the message, they might reconsider. Then again, they also might write off the whole thing as a hoax. Fran shrugged. Each person had to believe on his own accord. Except for Ted. She *had* to make Ted believe.

Hearing the femmes discuss the Rebel reminded her of some more work she needed to handle, so after procuring a large frosty drink, Fran moved to her and Pete's old meeting bench and slid another DJ from her boot. Well-trained Rebels learned the hunt went best when conditions, such as a crowded lunchtime Agora, allowed them to go unnoticed. Fran knew if she lingered by a vent, she'd run across a few like-minded brothers.

After a short wait, she heard the old familiar hum and perceived movement behind the plastic palm. Fran waited until the Rebel secured himself into the safety of the fold, a few feet from where she sat, before trying to catch his attention.

"Psst."

He looked up and held her stare. Fran cringed at his rookie mistake. *Eyes down.* Sure, she wanted to get his attention, but a well-trained Rebel knew better than to stare. That's how the beginners got caught.

Fran laid the DJ onto the floor and placed her boot on top of it. While holding the stare, she launched it across the floor, landing it at his feet. The Rebel's eyes lit up. He bent down and snatched up the device. Fran placed her smoothie onto the bench and walked away.

.~.

The Waltonian, perched high above the Agora on its own premiere pedestal revolved in a slow circle, affording a glimpse of the cityscape to chic diners. Fran sat in a fancy, velvet chair listening to the excited clucking of residents on the far side as their windows snuck past the Council's Viewing Loft. Of course, the loft remained empty at the moment, but the crowd seemed titillated, nonetheless. A commingling of disgust for the nonsense mixed with sadness for these people.

A waiter dressed in a black tuxedo appeared at her table. Not an overly enthusiastic, pixilated Graphie but a flesh-and-blood man, complete with a white linen draped over his arm.

Fran smiled. "I'm still waiting for my guest."

"Excellent, mademoiselle. Would you care for a sparkling cider or perhaps a smooth elixir while you wait?"

"Sure. Cider, please."

So what was she going to say? *"Hey Ted, I saw Mom and Dad. They said you should come home."*

That probably wouldn't fly. Of course, her reputation for being a reasonable sister had been lost awhile back. Yet, she *had* relinquished Rebel status. Would that be enough to convince him? Did she dare just whip out the DJ and say, *"Hey take a look at this, bro."*

On one hand, she wished she had a more solid plan. On the other? Maybe a well-thought proposal might have sounded too contrived anyway.

The waiter placed a long-stemmed glass onto the table and poured the sparkly beverage. Fran watched the bubbles scatter about the liquid, all frantic and wayward, doing an imperfect dance. She lifted the glass to her lips and experienced the sting of fizz.

Ted showed up a moment later. "Who's paying for this one?"

Fran smiled. "Your baby sister, of course."

The waiter pulled out a chair for Ted, and he slid in across from Fran. "I'm impressed."

Fran released a nervous laugh. "Yes, I'm working for a Superior now."

She figured it wasn't a *total* lie since Doc had been a Superior at one time. Ted responded with a nod and chuckle.

"Aren't we all?"

"Ted, you don't think I'm crazy, do you?"

He cocked an eyebrow. "Listen, Wickworm, I know life has dealt you a few blows. I know you were really close to Mom. I miss her too, you know. I understand the reason for your rebellion. But—"

"But what?" Fran stared at her brother in disbelief. *Too bad, so sad. Move on, little sis.*

"But nothing." Ted looked down at the linen napkin and placed it onto his lap before returning his attention to his sister. "You were saying?"

"The Epoch. It's here."

Ted's eyes shot open before he leaned back in his chair and laced his fingers behind his head.

"Nice one. You almost had me."

"No, really."

"And you know this how?"

Fran heard the resonance of Nissa's influence and hated the way Ted looked down his nose at her. She remembered the words her father had said just a few nights ago at the river. This world had become Ted's oyster. He'd found his treasure and had surrendered his personal search for truth. She wanted to scream, wanted to shake him. She wanted to grab him by the hand and drag him to the secret venting, shove him between the mammoth blades and into the open air.

Instead, she held her breath to allow the wave of grief to pass. Then with a phony laugh, she added, "Just kidding."

Ted chuckled. "Same old Wickworm, huh?" He held up his own glass of sparkling cider. "Welcome back, little sister."

"Thanks." Fran took a sip of the fizzy drink. "So, here's a hypothetical question for you."

Ted nodded for her to continue as he dipped focaccia into a pool of infused oils.

"What if the Epoch *was* here? And… what if Mom and Dad were alive out there somewhere?"

Ted laughed and crumbs from his bread spilled onto his chest. "Sure. And what if Graphies could have babies."

"Good one, Ted. Baby Graphies." Fran parroted his laugh and took another sip of juice as he brushed the crumbs from shirt.

"But if they were alive, wouldn't you want to know?"

"Yes, of course."

Fran felt a moment of hope.

"And I'd also like to know how a Graphie managed to make a baby."

He wiggled his brows and winked at his sister. A sickness settled deep into her gut. Fran redirected the conversation to more mundane matters and everyday gossip as she tried to think of a different angle. Something that would help her brother see the light. As they continued their meal, futility coursed through her body. Like poison dripping into her veins, every off-handed comment and rude gesture from this guy who *looked* like her brother seemed to destroy her hope. The Council, or Nissa, or *somebody* had stolen the real Ted and replaced him with this imposter—a West Wing sellout.

The restaurant continued to revolve, and soon, they turned just a few feet away from the Superior Viewing Loft. Hushed exaltations and giddy excitement grew from neighboring tables. Fran didn't bother to look. She couldn't give honor to the ones who held her brother in their invisible clutches. Yet, something flickered in Ted's eye—a sudden gleam of surprise—and she lifted her gaze with the others.

The Council had arrived and taken their seats.

What in the world?

"I wonder what's going on. Want to check it out?" Ted asked.

Before Fran could answer, her brother, along with a dozen other Waltonian patrons, rose and moved to a nearby balcony. Fran followed, three steps behind, unsure she wanted to be party to what might be in the works. A few impatient residents elbowed past her, hoping to get the perfect ringside seat. Ted lifted a hand and waved to her over the crowd, but Fran looked away, satisfied with her back-row view.

As she looked out over the Agora, she spied Graphies corralling pedestrians to the East Court, leaving the stage and surrounding area barren. A crackling spike of electricity circulated through the air, and a Graphie, several times larger than the average man, appeared center stage. A hush fell over the court.

"My fellow Impervieites, we come to you today with sad news."

A wave of chatter moved through the crowd. The people around Fran speculated as to what might have happened.

"An extreme act of treasonous terror has been committed within our city walls. We know it to be the act of a troubled soul. One swept up into the arms of a dangerous coup d'état."

Loud gasps and hissing *tsks* trailed throughout the restaurant. A moment later, a ratty Rebel, the same one she had seen earlier, was brought to the stage. Fran stood paralyzed while visions of the DJ sliding across the floor and an untouched smoothie flashed through her brain. The Graphie droned on. His words rebounded off the high ceilings and echoed throughout the Agora. "We have asked ourselves, how do we handle this treachery? What is good and proper?"

Fran's heart rattled hard and fast.

"We have decided to treat rebellion with love. What the Rebels meant for evil, we will use for good. We have chosen the most dignified of endings for this man."

Boy! Fran's heart cried out in silence. *He's not a man, he's a boy. Just a boy!*

A femme in an iridescent gown moved forward and cloaked the rebel in a velvety robe.

No! Fran choked on her own terror.

The Rebel stared straight ahead, not even squirming, and Fran realized he had already been poisoned. The femme led him down the stairs and off the stage, and one small boy in a big velvety robe began a silent parade. She knew his slippers swished. She also knew how this single Rebel procession was bound to end.

Fran turned and ran.

Out of the Waltonian. Through the back hallways of the West Wing and along the bridge that joined East and West.

In her mind, the screaming never ceased.

Chapter Twenty Five

Face down on her flip-flop, Fran lay in a tangle of sheets, weeping for the boy whose name she didn't even know and the brother being held hostage. Was it an impossible task? Was there hope for the truth? She wept for Fiona and Marie and the sickness that had stolen years from their lives. Cried out for Bob and John and the misery they still faced.

Fran wept until her soaked pillow clung to her face. Her eyes burned, and she lay on her bed listening to the silence, punctuated only by a throbbing in her temple.

Tomorrow.

Tomorrow, she would jump the truth onto as many readers as she could. Then she would watch Pete's hearing, walk with him to the Ranch, and, united, they would exit this hell.

And never come back.

.~.

The next morning, Fran spent a few hours in the Agora with her DJ's before heading off to the courtroom to catch Pete's trial. She elbowed her way to the front of the crowded civilian viewing loft. *Another slow day in the city.*

She ran a finger along the names on the docket until she came to Pete's case—fourth in line. She spotted him down on the hearing floor, awaiting his turn looking trendy and chic in a plaid kilt. *Nice touch, Pete.*

Fran noticed his muscular legs. She'd never seen them unveiled before, and their definition surprised her. It made sense, of course. All of the crawling and climbing? Great lower body workouts. She admired the way he sat—tall and confident. A flicker of warmth returned to her belly. With the ample time afforded outside, she did look forward to getting to know him a little better. Maybe tonight they'd sit by the fire, and she'd introduce Pete to her Mom and Dad. Holy cow... and what about Pete's parents!? She'd completely forgotten about them. How long ago had they declined? Were they at Village Number One, or had they ventured off? An easy smile meandered across her face as she considered the reunions.

When the trials began, she listened with partial interest. The first defendant had hoarded. Apparently, of the 100,000 lifetime meal credits, he'd only used 5,000. Fran looked at the full figure even a pleated kilt couldn't hide. Obviously, this guy had not starved himself. Total moocher.

Sentencing? A charge of 50,000 meal credits and a strict warning to eat three meals a day. A woman in the front row cried. *Seriously?*

Defendant number two: Slothfulness. According to Impervious Entitlement Law, adequate food, housing, and—depending upon family money line—spending credits imparted to each resident allowed for a comfortable life. However, Community Service credits, a system devised to encourage and reward volunteer work, also played into the culture. Child-minders, the work Fran's mom did, fell into this under-paid category. Fran didn't know if one credit had been equated the same dollar amount from the ancient, pre-war era, but it didn't matter. In most cases, when the family money ran out, a resident joined the ranks of Community Service workers—which made up most of the East Wing.

Yet, even though those with family money still rolling around their accounts didn't need to dirty their hands on a daily basis, slothfulness was discouraged. So much so, a law had been put in place requiring every Accountable person over the age of thirteen to work at least one hour per week or be in violation of slothfulness. Fran remembered caring for the juvies at the ICS with her mother and loved the few hours a week she'd donated. The job gave her something to look forward to. A purpose.

An hour a *week* to donate to a worthy cause. Why would anyone break that law? In her mind, loads of words described *that* type of person, and none of them included the politically-correct term of slothfulness. She hoped they found a suitable penance for this one. She listened to the case and couldn't help but roll her eyes as the trendy West Winger whined to the judging panel over why she hadn't been able to fulfill her Community Service obligation for the last half year. Her body hugging dress shimmered as she lifted her hands in exasperation. Embarrassing cleavage revealed more skin than Fran cared to see as the girl continued her spectacle for the sour looking crony. *At least he's not sleeping this time.* Finally, the committee announced punishment: Two hours of Community Service per week until a penance of ten total hours had been paid.

Chatter rose in the viewing loft as residents pooh-poohed the ruling. Then again, they came for the show, so in reality, Fran figured they were satisfied with the entertainment.

Defendant number three: Xenophobia.

Considered a hate crime, this offense carried quite a bit more weight, and the Council exercised zero tolerance. They claimed this attitude to be the cornerstone of hate that led to the final war — a fight cloaked in prejudice and racism. The Council considered the act of intolerance so serious that upon reaching the Age of Accountability, each resident signed a witnessed document proclaiming to uphold the dignity of his brother.

The Signing, commemorated in sixth grade and most parents hosted big parties with hot hors d'oeuvres after the recitation of The Oath. *"In no way will I judge, assume malice, or undermine the ideals and freedoms of my fellow man. As I hold dear my own personal truths, so does my brother. Therefore, for the sake of harmony and peace under our single metal dome, we shall not impose our beliefs upon our brothers."*

Fran snorted. She, Mom, and Ted had gone out for a celebratory ice cream after her recitation.

Defendant number three had caused a riot after a night at the pub, slurring the ideals of West Wingers and calling them frauds and sellouts. *Ouch. That one stung.* His sentencing? A penance of 100 hours of Community Care, cleaning the residences of the very ones he had insulted. How ironic. That ought to knock the xeno right out from under his phobia.

After an eternity, Pete's turn arrived. Fran wiggled in her seat and glanced at her com device. She had thirty minutes before her start time at the Ranch. Her boot drummed on the floor.

Judge number One began the questioning. "Peter Katigoruminous. You have been found Unaccountable. What is your response?"

Fran chewed her nails as she waited for Pete to answer. After an uncomfortable pause, Pete stood.

"I was Unaccountable. I lived as a Rebel."

"Yes, Mr. Katigoruminous. We already established your Unaccountability. Do you have anything to add to that? We would like to try to understand your reasoning before we assign penance."

"Because I don't like the mandates of the Council."

Gasps rang out from the loft, and a hum of chatter arose. Fran halted mid-nail. She leaned forward in her chair.

"Mr. Katigoruminous, to what mandates are you referring?"

"All of them. Accountability being number one."

"Rabble rouser." A women seated near Fran sneered as her eyes lit with delight.

Her companion added his thoughts. "Such insolence."

His eyes flicked to either side, and he pursed his thin lips as if to contain his satisfaction.

Judge number two, the Superior, sat up in his chair.

"Mr. Katigor…" The judge bumbled before baling on Pete's surname. "Peter, please tell us why you find Accountability to be unjust."

Fran stared at the back of Pete's head trying to send him mental messages. *Stop! Just take your punishment, and we'll be home free.*

"Because my life is none of the Council's business. I should be free to choose where I live, how often I eat…" His voice softened, and Fran leaned in. "And who I kiss."

Her face heated. A tear threatened, and she pulled in her breath, holding it tight in her chest.

The Superior cleared his throat. "Yes, I can see why your kissing should be a private matter. However, Peter, it is, in fact, of great importance to the Council where you live, etc. We find that to be the very thread that sews order into our home."

"Our home?" Pete laughed. "More like prison."

Jeers and hisses rang out from the civilian viewing loft. Names like *traitor* and *fugitive* bounced off the walls of the courtroom. Claws of mortification scratched at Fran's soul.

What is he doing? This isn't anything like Pete. What's happening?

"Thank you, Peter. That is all I have." Judge number two sat back.

The third Judge squinted his eyes. Fran saw evil glint from the center. Something was wrong. Somehow they had gotten to Pete. Her brain jumbled, and she wanted to vomit. She had to help Pete but had no idea how.

"Peter, because of an item found on your person today, we have reason to believe you may be party to a coup d'état. Please respond."

"Coup d'état?" Pete laughed again.

The viewing platform grew silent. Fran looked to her right and to her left. She saw fear. Not the usual fear of the decline, or even a fear of this outspoken Rebel for that matter, but something new. They sensed a shift in the order they had always known. The birth of a new terror — even uglier than the one kept hidden in their vaults. The fear only acknowledged in small doses.

"Yes, Mr. Katigoruminous, a coup d'état. An effort to overthrow the work of the Council. How do you respond?"

"The Council is this city's worst enemy." Pete turned around and faced the viewing loft. "Brothers and sisters, I implore you to look beyond the things that can be seen. I beg of you to seek the truth."

Fran mouthed the word *Stop*!

The Graphie had already materialized beside Pete with enough power to send its electromagnescence into the loft. Static electricity lifted the tiny hairs on Fran's skin.

Pete stared straight into Fran's eyes. And then he dropped to the floor.

Chapter Twenty Six

Fran sat frozen in the loft, hands clamped over her mouth to stop the scream that tried to burst forth. The viewing loft emptied of onlookers after a few city workers hauled a half-baked Pete to Holding. The face of the nameless Rebel haunted her thoughts. Would they do the same thing to Pete? What could she do to help him? Stage a rescue mission? One Wolf against the Council? Hah!

She couldn't just do nothing. But what? Without even feeling her own legs move, Fran rushed out of the courtroom to the nearest venting. A code entry, the hum of the cover, a headfirst dive, and utter darkness—an abyss as deep as the night sky with no moon or stars to light the way.

The tightness of space and blinding darkness sent a wave of claustrophobia through her body. Panic rose in her chest, and spiky pins moved down her legs like the very first time Chan led her through the short maze. She could hear his voice.

Calm down, Wolf. You got this.

She closed her eyes and tapped her finger, breathing in the dusty essence as she listened to the creaking and moaning. The schematics blossomed in her brain. She lifted onto hands and knees and began to skulk to the land of the Superiors.

Her head spun with memories of the last time she and Pete had spied on these hallowed halls. The idea came about after a day of sleeping and eating, when their boredom spurred on the idea of a midnight tunnel run. Fran choked back a weepy snort as she remembered Pete's strange combination of fear and giddiness and the ditty he'd made up to honor their outing.

Cronies, Top-Dogs, Velvet coats,
Faces look like mother goats,
Eau de Crony fills your hallowed halls,
And the same smell lurks in the bathroom stalls...

Fran hummed the tune, and a tear trailed down her cheek and dripped onto the metal. She snaked through the tunnels, trying to keep her mind clear. Too many outside thoughts equaled confusion. Confusion equaled chaos. And chaos? Failure.

She zigzagged her way up to the top floor and approached the super-long shaft that crossed the Agora. Suspended from the ceiling with thick wires, the tunnel swayed ever-so-slightly as she moved. The hustle and bustle from below echoed through the pipe, creating a maddening mix of noise. Between the sounds of confusion and the blinding darkness, she fell prey to the odd sense of unsteadiness that always accompanied this quarter-mile stretch.

Once across, she moved past the land of cybernetic vacation pods and caught glimpses of sandy seashores, virtual ski slopes, and evening gondola rides in the canals of Venice. Finally, she traversed the perimeter of the lobby to the Council Offices.

This air smelled different than the surrounding businesses, but not like Pete implied with his witty lyrics. More like a sort of musty, peppery smell. It looked different than the rest of the city too. Antique, plump furnishings weighed down the thick carpets, so different from the sharp angles and glistening acrylic furniture that spoke of modern day. Some sort of antiquated music emanated from hidden speakers.

She moved past the mismatched desks of the staffers and small offices of the lower ranking Superiors. To date, two-hundred cronies who had 'avoided the plague' made up the Council — the ones with such exceptional DNA they lived past the standard shortened life span.

Fran wondered if the Council members even knew of the sham or if they believed themselves to be genetically superior. The Seven, made up of Marcus and The Sons of the Generations as well as four of Marcus' closest cohorts, were the big dogs. The revered ones. Genetically *and* politically superior. The thought nauseated Fran.

The Council Meeting Chamber sat behind the wall of offices in a mix of velvet, leather, and glossy wood. Smells of pipe-tobacco and hard liquor filled the air. Hundreds of high-backed chairs surrounded a central platform. Fran scurried past the first venting and took a few turns until she maneuvered to an optimal viewing space.

After a few quick minutes, a crony entered the room, holding a reader and mumbling, in conversation to a cohort. She couldn't tell what they discussed, but then again, she really didn't care. From the red suit jackets, she knew these guys weren't the high rankers on the food chain—probably mid-hierarchy. If she remembered correctly from Social Studies, staffers wore green, middle-management red, and the top dogs—all black.

Just another visual opportunity for Marcus to assert status. As she waited, more and more red jackets filled the room. Some wandered about, greeting buddies with a hard slap on the back. Others sat in chairs examining readers or nodding off. Then, a hush fell upon the room, and the sea of red parted as a line of black jackets snaked through the center.

Marcus, the final man to enter, looked even more gruesome up close than Fran had imagined. Gravity wrestled with the skin on his face, pulling everything downward. Hundreds of lines meandered through leathery cheeks, and the sparse white hair on his head reminded Fran of wispy cotton. His rounded shoulders and jutting head created the illusion of a hunchback as he shuffled into the room and took his place on the platform. For the briefest of moments, Fran felt sorry for this pathetic man. Until he opened his mouth to speak.

"Members of the Council, please be seated."

A shuffling ensued, followed by reverent silence. After a lengthy pause, Marcus continued.

"I will get right to the point. Two Unaccountable Rebels have been captured within the last forty-eight hours. Each Rebel had a DataJump on his person. After closer investigation, the DataJumps were found to contain notes from the life of Dr. Benjamin Leiben, our fallen brother."

Mumblings and chatter rose from the sea of red coats, and Marcus waited for the wave to settle before he continued.

"As you know, Benjamin was a close friend of mine. One of the original creators of Impervious. However, poor Ben didn't possess the same wherewithal of those of us gathered in this room. Too many years underground changed him, and he commenced with a rebellious behavior that still festers in our bunker today."

Two hundred heads nodded and murmured their agreement.

"We can't let his words infect our city. We must erase the existence of this madness. And I do believe I hold the key."

Marcus nodded to his closest cohort, and the doors of the Council Chamber whooshed open. Fran gasped before she could clamp a hand over her mouth. Two guards ushered in Pete—bound and gagged, eyes bulging with fear.

"What we have here, Council Members, is an official Rebel rat." Marcus' venom spewed into the room. "Just like his brother from yesterday, he will be used to display to the city the fate of those who oppose the Council. Marcus clasped his hands together as if in prayer, and words hissed through tight lips.

"My subordinates have been working a technology I'm sure you will find as delightful as I have." He laughed. "And, the Rebels have nothing. No weapons, and certainly no leader who could battle against us. I daresay, unless every single Rebel came forth and stormed the stage, the group has no recourse."

Marcus' gaze rested on the vent. Fran could have sworn his aged eyes locked onto her own for the briefest of moments.

"Please present yourselves to the viewing loft at 1400. I think you'll be interested to see what I have in store."

Fran clamped her lids and leaned deeper into the shadows of the pipe. Was her mind playing tricks on her? Like when she had assumed Retter to be a cannibal? Or did Marcus somehow know of her presence? With eyes shut tight, she inched backwards and then scurried deeper into the tunnel. Marcus didn't think the Rebels shared the common thread of unity? Fran begged to differ. She maneuvered back through the venting, fashioning a plan that would blow the Council's dirty socks right off their knobby feet.

She moved to the first point. The place Folsom always camped near the East side of the Agora. No yellow light illuminated his space and Fran panicked. *Please be sleeping, Folsom.*

She plowed into him. He yelped and growled.

"Folsom. It's me, Wolf."

"Wolf? I thought you were back on the grid."

"I am."

"Oh really?" Folsom chuckled. "I like you, Wolf. You're always up to something."

"Listen, I'm here for Pete."

"Prankster Pete? I heard you and him—"

Fran interrupted. "—Folsom. *Listen* to me." She wanted to shake him but opted for a deep breath. "Pete's in trouble. I have a feeling if we don't step up, we're going to lose him to the Council. We need everyone on board. Round up the Rebels from Zones One through Six. I'll get the rest and meet you back here."

As Fran inched backwards, she heard a soft snore. She banged on the metal with her boot.

"Folsom. *Now.*"

Fran scurried off banging the metal walls and whooping through venting. It was a siren of sorts. One her Rebel brothers would recognize. As she reached the first "T" she heard responsive banging.

"Sound off," she demanded, just like Chan used to.

"Offrey," The Rebel stated. "What's with the excitement?"

"They've got Pete, Offrey. We need everyone to come together."

A lighter tapping announced another Rebel.

"It's Derrick," a voice shouted before being addressed.

"Newbie?" Fran inquired.

"Yes." Offrey and Derrick's voices collided.

"I'm putting you guys in charge of the Southeast sector. Grab everyone you can and meet me back here in one hour."

A short time later, a heavy sweat ran down Fran's back as she moved. A dozen rebels moved in line behind her. Would this plan even work? At least Marcus had sounded afraid it might. Every petitioned Rebel had joined the cause. Julias, Fenwick, and Jasmine she knew. The rest of those behind her, were new, however. It didn't matter. Everyone loved Pete. He'd made a name for himself in a very short time—his laughter like balm on weary Rebel hearts.

They met up with Folsom at the large "T" right by the East Side, and the group moved as a unit into the HVAC Systems Hub—a land of twisting tubes, mammoth fans, and the one-ton filtration system. The space was loud and crowded. Fran arrived first and stood by as each and every Rebel exited the pipe. The mood of the Rebels seemed a bit off putting.

"What are we here for?" Fenwick snipped.

"I don't know," said another. "I just followed you all here."

Jasmine rolled out of the vent and readjusted her snug tank. "I hope there's food."

Fran waited until they had all exited before climbing onto an elevated shaft. She counted thirty-one Rebels total, including herself and Folsom. Would it be enough? If they stormed the stage, would they outnumber the available Graphies? At least they had the element of surprise on their side. She shouted out to the assembly.

"Thank you for coming everyone. In case you haven't been told, we're gathering today to help a fellow Rebel fight the Council."

"Prankster Pete, right?" A voice called out from the throng.

"Yes. Prankster Pete." Fran smiled. "He made us laugh, so how about we return the favor?"

An unexpected silence followed. Then Derrick shouted out. "But we'll be risking house arrest right?"

"That's insanity," another Rebel added.

Soon, the rest of the crowd began to raise their voices and Fran couldn't be heard. She looked at her downtrodden, rag-tag brothers and sisters. She'd been where they are and understood… they were hungry, and tired, and feared the Council.

Fran also realized she had the advantage. She now knew what the fight was for — blue skies, fresh air, green grass and flowers. Breezes that tickled her cheek and fresh water that tasted strange, but had the power to heal. And just as the refreshing dip in the warm springs had renewed her spirit, knowing she was being given a new life, free to live with the ones she loved most? Well it was like being born all over again. She'd witnessed the truth and knew without a doubt what awaited above ground. They, however, had yet to witness the Epoch.

She squatted low on the pipe and pounded on the metal. She shrieked her loudest, "whoop!" All eyes rose to her perch. As the chatter died, Fran dug deep into her soul — deeper than her fear, and around her typical sarcasm — and felt the spirit of her mentor rise.

"We are not gathered today to wage a war but rather to stop the battle of insanity that has raged on far too long." She yelled to be heard over the fans. "We have no weapons. We have nothing to our names, but I have news for you, brothers and sisters."

Fran took a deep breath and shouted, "The Epoch has arrived. The air is clean, and our suffering is almost over."

Murmurs rose like a wave, and Fran continued. "I tell you, truly, I have seen it. I have walked upon the green grasses and felt the warm sun on my shoulders."

A few gasps rang out, and a handful of questions shot forth.

"Were there any Geiger ghosts?"

"Was the sky gray and cold?"

"How did you get out?"

"Are you contaminated?"

"I know you must have a million questions. I know because I did before I saw it with my own eyes. But you must take it on faith. The open-air is safe. It is bright, alive, and will blow your mind. True healing awaits us out there, and that, my brothers and sisters, is the truth. Though the Council may have the ability to harm our flesh; they cannot take the truth from us. Stand firm in that knowledge as we move forth and see this to victory. When Pete is in our midst, we will all walk out of this place, and we will be healed. We are equipped with the truth, and we must wear it like armor as we face the Council. Remember, we are not here to harm the people of this city but to disarm the evil that holds us all hostage. We are heirs to the world, brothers and sisters. Although we may stand here as outcasts and paupers, this earth was bought and paid for by our ancestors."

The Rebels whooped with excitement, and Fran smiled. Her plan would work. It *had* to work.

Chapter Twenty Seven

Fran waited with her cheek pressed against the venting and scanned the courts. A quick glance cross-court to venting A62 revealed a flicker of light as the eyes of a Rebel-brother blinked. She peeled her tongue from the roof of her dry mouth.

A commotion overhead captured her attention. They had come. Her stomach tightened. A small part of her hoped her overactive imagination had fabricated the whole thing. Panic began to rise. *Focus Wolf.*

A moment later, it began. Like all processions of the Council, Graphies and electrical fencing herded the throng of Impervieites from their activities in the West Court to the already crowded East Court. Once the entire West Court floor had been cleared, an enormous Graphie appeared in the center, his voice thundered while saluting the Superiors and then welcoming the awaiting audience.

That's when she saw him.

On the stage.

In a velvety robe and whisper-soft slippers.

The scene unfolded like a dream as her mind attempted to disengage itself from the terrifying reality. Flashes of memories, like clips from a movie trailer, played out in another realm where time did not exist. The arching of his eyebrow, the sound of his howl, chocolate covered peanuts, and turkey sandwiches all melded together into one emotional collage before pulling apart with vivid clarity. Her throat closed up as she remembered his warm breath and the way he'd whispered her name.

Not Wolf.

Not Fran.

But Sarah, her real name.

Fran flashed her old Light-Genie to cue her team. She was certain the Council would take notice when every venting slid open. She, at least, had prepared to hear shouts from onlookers as thirty-one rebels exited their vents and into the barren courts. What she hadn't anticipated as she slithered from the darkness, was hearing Pete's shout from the stage.

"Wolf. Go back!"

Her feet froze in place, and her head turned to view the expanse of the Agora. It didn't make sense. Not a single pixilated presence or computer generated voice declared each Rebel become Accountable. Yet, every tiny hair on Fran's body rose, and her head buzzed with an intense electromagnetic manifestation.

Overhead lights dimmed, and a holographic scene unfolded. The smooth flooring of the shopping courts morphed into a desert-like terrain—just like the scene when she watched Nissa perform *Mission Perdition* for Ted. The Lunch Hut became a jagged butte with sharp rocks jutting out from its face. Hot wind burned her cheeks while pelting sand blew through the air. Artificial warmth engulfed her body. Her hands glowed.

"Ladies and Gentleman. Welcome to the Desert!" The voice boomed through the court and echoed off of the high ceiling.

"Tonight's debut performance, brought to you by way of the Council, will be the ultimate in the gaming experience. Be prepared to go to the brink. Ready yourself for the show of a lifetime. You will find yourself on the edge of your seat as fantasy becomes reality and reality turns to fantasy."

Fran's mind reeled as every Rebel lit up like a glowing Graphie. A gritty substance scratched at her skin. She rubbed the heated surface and recognized the smell of magnetized dust, an element she'd been allowed to view, but not touch, on her sixth-grade field trip to The Inventor's Wing. Besides that trip with her classmates, she'd never seen the element that turned a live man into a gaming avatar, getting rid of controllers and screens.

She had heard this new phase of gaming technology to be underway. Up until this moment, however, she'd thought it was no more than a hopeful rumor. Yet now highly-charged metallic receptacles attached to her skin. And, now, she had become the game.

Although from her vantage point, Fran clearly recognized each Rebel enshrouded within the glow of their gaming character, she realized that on the video screens and to the spectators watching from the balconies, they all appeared to be nothing more than gaming pieces.

Thirty-one vents hummed closed as Zombies pixelated in the court—dreadful holographs with open wounds and rotted flesh. Fetid odors surged through the courts; their shrieks and groans became a nightmarish audio backdrop as the announcer continued.

"Tonight, the battle of Behemoth and Queen Xyphon continues, as well as the fight between the dead and the Unaccountable. The Queen will rule with the Zombies, and the dreaded Behemoth will wreak havoc with the Rebels. Sit back and enjoy the entertainment as we present to you, *Mission Perdition II–Nightmare of a Rebel.*"

Music sounded as the words "Mission Perdition II" floated through the air.

This can't be happening. Fran's head whipped from side to side. A few Rebels scurried back to the openings from where they had emerged. Fran shook herself from the shock-inflicted paralysis. Fight or flight—a human instinct as basic as breathing—overtook her senses. She back ran to her venting exit and swiped in the code.

Nothing.

Her hands shook. Maybe she swiped the wrong numbers. She tried again.

The grating remained stone cold. Unmoving. Locked up tight. She looked around as her comrades struggled to return to the safety of a vent. They scurried as they tried to dodge the ethereal light draped over them.

She looked up at the Viewing Loft. An opaque shield acted as a buffer between the Superiors and the courts. And the cheering crowd? They believed this spectacle to be yet another gaming experience. Death didn't exist in this make-believe world.

About twenty-five feet away, Derrick, huddled against his venting pounding on the opening with balled fists. His face contorted, and his mouth moved as he screamed. The crowd cheered when growls of death rang out from the hidden speakers, drowning out his desperate cries.

A grisly, yellow-faced Zombie lunged at her Rebel brother and covered him in a mound of snarls and rotting flesh. Holographic blood squirted out from beneath the Zombie, painting a nearby wall with red pixilations.

Fran's heart stopped. *But it's not real.* She closed her eyes. *It's not real. None of this is real.* She repeated it over and over. Maybe, in their insane minds, the Council believed they could use the Rebels as human avatars, but Fran knew it took more than holographic teeth and claws to kill a real man.

Even so, when the zombie stepped away, Derrick remained on the ground in a helpless pile. Unmoving. A pixilated stream of blood trickled from his body.

Fran screamed, "Derrick, get up!"

Her cries couldn't be heard over the surrounding roar as the crowd went wild. The zombie lifted two hands over his head in the sign of victory as he lumbered away from Derrick, toward Fran.

"Derrick, get up!" She screamed the command over and over as she raced toward his body. As she lifted her hand, a spade pixilated in the air as if she held it. It stayed with her as she ran, and right when she moved past the zombie, the spade came down onto his head. When it sunk, a deep, gloppy, squishing sound heralded through the speakers. Holographic gray matter oozed, leaving Fran sick to her stomach. *It's not real; it's not real.*

She continued running blindly toward Derrick and almost collided with Folsom as they both made the approach. Derrick still lay unmoving. *He can't be dead. It was just a holograph.*

She smelled it first—the odor of seared flesh. Her gaze locked on his body. He remained wide-eyed as if in shock. His arms jerked once or twice, and his legs followed suit, giving Fran a moment of hope. Yet, as she neared, she saw the absence of breath— no rise or fall of his chest. And a soft coil of smoke as it rose from Derrick's body.

He had been cooked… from the inside out.

She gagged, threw her hand over her mouth and nose, and shuffled backwards, aware his body still teemed with a lethal dose of electricity.

Folsom reached out to him.

"Stop!" she screeched, but her warning was too late. The wave moved through Derrick's body and lashed out at Folsom like a viper. While glued to Derrick, Folsom shook with unseen power, unable to release the hold. His legs thrashed, his back arched, and his head flopped.

Stop! Just stop! Fran's lips didn't move as she screamed at the Beast.

A wave of excitement lifted from the surrounding structures. Cheers and whistles rang out from the four corners. Behemoth swept in. With the grace of a hawk, he grabbed a zombie with his vice-like claws. The zombie squirmed and moaned, and an explosion of holographic zombie body parts littered the desert-like sky.

A female droid voice hummed through the speakers. "Xyphon, twenty points. Behemoth, twenty points."

Fran looked around the courts. Already piles of fallen Rebels and random pixilated zombie-parts, littered the holographic landscape. The winged avatar circle overhead and dove into the ring. She knew, at this very moment, Nissa sat in her simulated gaming chair, whooping and hollering every time a zombie went down. Did she even know the Rebels were real? And what about Ted? Was he at home cheering on his bride with the same crazy enthusiasm as the live crowd? At least she and Nissa were on the same side of the fight this time.

In one swoop, Behemoth took out two zombies. Just Nissa's way of showing off. The audience roared. Some cheered while others booed and hissed. Then, a display of flashing lights drew attention to the main stage where Pete still stood, a world away from where Fran fought for her life in the courts. With much fanfare, a well-dressed guard ushered Pete away. Fran called out his name but knew he couldn't hear. Was he already poisoned? Would he fall into the spasm of death as soon as he left her sight?

The stage transformed into a palatial throne room with walls of gold and gem-encrusted adornments. A silky white robe and an endless flowing train filled the throne room as the Queen pixilated to life. Thick, black tresses cascaded over her robe. The ends wiggled and hissed. A hundred pairs of gleaming eyes peeked out from the depths. Razor-sharp facial features and blood-red lips shimmered into view.

One word took shape in Fran's mind: *Wicked.* Queen Xyphon moved with dignity and power as she climbed onto her elevated throne. From her pedestal, she became all-seeing, all-knowing. Her loud voice trumpeted through the speakers.

"Not one Rebel shall go unaccounted tonight. The blood will run deep, and the city will be cleansed of the rats that wander in a cloak of darkness. Zombies, you have been commissioned to do my work. I now bestow upon you the gift of speed."

A nearby lumbering zombie broke into a full run. Fran's heart raced. She had sprinted through the Agora plenty of times with ease. And tonight, with an overload of hot adrenaline, she was bound to break her old speed records. But would that be enough for human versus avatar?

Fran raced cross-court and moved behind the opaque, rocky outline engulfing The Lunch Hut. The zombie stopped running. *Seriously? You can't see me?* She must have been losing her mind because for a *millionth* of a second, it all seemed comical.

Behemoth soared overhead and the zombie had no place to hide. A moment later, zombie parts littered the arena. Down to eleven. From her hiding place, Fran scanned the court and counted the heaps of her fallen Rebels. Her heart broke as she counted past ten, eleven, and twelve. She closed her eyes, unable to process the loss. The sounds of screams and groans accosted her ears. The high voltage waves bit at her skin like prickly barbs. The odor of burning flesh ignited her old memory of advanced HAZMAT and the swirling ashes of humanity. Imagining air tainted with the charred DNA of her comrades, Fran choked on her own breath. She needed an immediate place of peace. Maybe she should just show her face and let the zombie finish her off.

She pushed back tears as her mind went to the open air, to her mother and the love that had always rained down from her heart. She thought of her father and the short time they spent together. Fran pictured the vivid night sky and the light of the moon. She thought about Ted, how they had romped through the hallways trying to outrun the RIT's when they were kids.

She reflected back to her learning years and the project in Englehardt's class that garnered her an 'A' for the entire semester…collision rate of plasma energy. Her mind halted on that thought. She remembered Englehardt's stern warning to the class after she had presented her findings.

"*Just remember, kids. That much impact would also have the ability to produce a synergistic blackout. Not something to be taken lightly.*"

Could it work? Could she force the hand of the Queen and destroy her entire army in one fell swoop? Fran felt certain she could draw them together if she had the right bait. Then she realized… *she* was the perfect bait.

She knew the lay of this land, had traversed the Agora under the radar more times than she could count on both hands. But could she do it in blinding darkness? A blackout would give her twelve seconds before an alternate power source rebooted. Could she get out in twelve seconds or less?

Fran peeked out from behind The Lunch Hut.

The Queen commanded.

The zombies ravaged.

Her comrades raced to and fro.

She hid herself within the light and edged around the perimeter of the Agora, making sure to stay within the illumination of the rocky walls. When she reached the stage, she crept up the stairway, and slithered to the center. Then, like a ridiculous avatar, Fran lifted to her full height and stood, hands-on-hips, staring at the animated Queen.

Queen Xyphon barked from her throne. "Who is this Rebel in my midst?"

Fran did not reply as she inched her way to the edge of the stage.

"Dare you sully my royal palace with your Rebel presence?" The evil voice rose in anger.

The cheers faded. Zombies stood at ease, and a hush fell over the courts. Behemoth landed in a corner and remained still. Even her remaining Rebel comrades stopped moving.

Fran assessed every nook, every cranny, every stationary object, and every hallway leading away from the courts. She knew exactly where to go. And she had the Queen's full attention.

Chapter Twenty Eight

The Queen bellowed from her throne, "Zombies, ravage this Rebel!"

That was her cue. Fran jumped from her elevated position on stage. Her eyes blurred as the nine remaining zombies raced cross court. She turned in a slow circle and watched as they approached the perimeter.

She drew in a deep breath, closed her eyes for a half a second, opened, and exhaled. The intense sensation engulfing her body made it hard to breathe. The zombies came close enough for her to make out their gruesome details — mangled faces and decaying flesh. Hair rose up from where it lay on her head. The prickliness morphed into a burn and then a stabbing, knife-like pain spread through her chest. A tear traveled down her cheek. The landscape blurred.

She closed her eyes, held her breath, placed her hands over her head, and curled up into a ball. Then with a moment-and-a-half between her and the nine holographs, a breath before they collided with one another and burst into a self-destructive power bomb, she hit the floor and rolled like a bowling ball away from the stage.

One somersault, two, three, and four. A crackle pierced the air as the surge of electricity consumed its own self, like a cannibalistic rat snake. The Agora lit up as if the sun had found its way inside the metal dome before it plunged into blinding, suffocating darkness.

At that moment, Fran began to count.

And run.

Chatter rose from the surrounding viewers.

One second.

She sprinted past the resting fountain, the smell of the rusty minerals surrounding her.

Two seconds.

She zigzagged past the stationary tables, their crumbly sandwich residue giving away an otherwise hidden location.

Three seconds.

Drawing a straight line in her head, she followed it like a beacon in the darkness.

Four seconds.

The heat from the moving stairway up ahead reached for her.

Five seconds.

She launched and stumbled as she climbed the frozen stairs two-at-a-time.

Six seconds.

Seven seconds.

Gripping the rubber railing, she pulled her weight to propel herself upward.

Eight seconds.

Reaching the landing, she felt the hard epoxy flooring.

Nine seconds.

She raced until she careened into the glass doors of the Le Petite Spa and used the hard, cold windows as a guide to move her to the hallway.

Ten seconds.

Eleven seconds.

The lights flickered.

She burst through the corridor, her throat and heart glued together with fear as she headed for the elevator.

Twelve seconds.

The crowd roared as the de-pixilated Agora came back to life. She imagined the cries came from the shock and repulsion as the crowd witnessed the littering of bodies across the epoxy flooring.

The doors of the elevator hummed closed. She jabbed the "S" button with her thumb. Her breath came in ragged sobs and agonizing wheezes. She clasped her chest, resting her head against the wall of the elevator.

By the time the elevator arrived at the Surface floor—Fran's breathing had almost normalized. Her throat and chest still burned from the thick EMP. The muscles in her arms and legs intermittently spasmed and twitched as they reeled from the intense magnetic overload. But she was alive. Just as Mr. Englehardt had warned, the power collision did produce the synergistic blackout, and the cloak of darkness had acted as her personal tunnel to escape the Agora. Darkness was a friend to every Rebel and she hoped they'd all used their twelve seconds as she had. *Just find a place to hide,* she thought. *I'll be back for you.*

The doors slid open, and Fran poked her head into the quiet vestibule. Were they scouring the hallways looking for her? Did they even know, Sarah Monde, had been in the Rebel crowd, or was she just one of thirty-one faceless Rebels? She still needed to get through the doors of the Ranch, but then after two lefts and a right she'd find her cover.

Fran looked down at her wrist.

My bangle!

It was gone.

How would she re-enter the Ranch? If she knocked on the door, Freddie or another guard would answer. Considering the deactivator plus showed her inside and at work, how would she explain? Fran had no doubts Freddie had watched the game on his reader. He'd figure it out. After all, she did kind-of have a history.

She would just have to wait it out. Sooner or later, someone would exit. Someone would leave for the day, and she would breeze through the door as they exited.

She crept through the hallway and sat on the bench outside of the facility—the one used by relatives of the post-primers as they waited for clearance. The one that stayed hidden behind a big phony ficus to block the distasteful view. She had no reason to fear, right? As far as the Council knew, her status showed Accountable, right?

The beady eyes of Marcus glaring into the venting haunted her imagination.

Just breathe.

She focused on her breath and closed her eyes.

Bad idea.

The gruesome faces of the Zombies filled her mind's eye, and the essence of charred bodies filled her nostrils. Her eyes popped open. She stared at the floor, working to block out what had transpired over the last few hours, nowhere near ready to process it all. Maybe she never would be. She hadn't gotten through to Ted. And what about Pete? She hadn't rescued Pete.

A sob lodged in her tight chest. So many Rebels had lost their lives. Fran felt her soul falling. The Beast. Failure. Hopelessness.

She remembered Marcus' cold stare as she watched from the venting. He had known. He'd used her like a pawn in his sick game. Maybe she should have never come back. Maybe she should just turn herself in and take the hit of a forfeiture.

Her mother's face came to mind, and a tear pinched the corner of her eye. Fran remembered the shriek that had erupted from her mother when their eyes had reconnected for the first time. The surprise and elation. The joy.

She's going to lose one son. Don't make her lose a daughter as well.

For her mother's sake, she had to go back. But not because she deserved to be free. She heard a thumping and Fran turned her head. John, one of the two remaining wards of Team-Fran, stood on the far side of the glass wall waving to her.

She laughed.

She cried.

As she stood to move toward the door, a buzzing filled her ears. She turned around just as an RIT zipped past. It stopped mid-air and circled around her head. She lifted her face. A flash of red. The RIT zoomed off. She continued toward the door, where John still waved, and smiled at her old friend. *So you do get up and walk around after all. Let's see what else you can do.*

Fran pointed to the door handle and mimed to John the motion for opening the door. John laughed. He didn't get it. Fran tried it again.

The hair on her arms began to rise, and a prickly sensation crawled upon her skin.

Huh?

It took longer than it should have for her to piece it all together. The RIT in a Surface floor hallway? And the electromagnescence of a Graphie? Had she forgotten their ways? Was her brain completely fried?

She looked back to John with renewed terror. The smile vanished from his face as he noticed the change. He looked down at his feet and began to shuffle away.

No!

Fran pounded on the glass. She shouted his name. She mimed the motion to open the door. *Please, John, please.*

Twelve seconds. She had twelve precious seconds to convince him, and she'd already wasted two. She bent down low so he could see her face as he gazed at his paper slippers. She caught his eye. She smiled and waved.

He smiled and waved.

She stood up.

He smiled and waved.

She mimed opening the door.

He opened the door.

She dove through the opening.

Chapter Twenty Nine

A Graphie materialized on the far side of the glass wall. Fran stared as the rippling holograph flashed red from his sockets before slowly de-pixilating to nothingness. She woofed out a breath and put her hands to her mouth as nausea rolled through her belly.

"Hi." John still smiled and waved.

"John, when you get outside, I'm going to give you a big kiss."

John puckered up.

"Oh. What the heck." Fran moved forward and planted a sloppy kiss on his lips.

John giggled. "I've got a girlfriend," he mumbled as he shuffled away.

Fran took a last, disbelieving, look over her shoulder and then sprinted down the hallway. She skidded to the left when she reached the first turn. Her head reeled and her heart beat much too fast. And too hard. Her eyes began to blur and she missed second left. Colliding with a wall, she slid to a stop and spun back around to the last hallway.

One more right, she reminded herself and soon saw the final turn up ahead. The swishing sound of paper booties filled her ears as she neared the supply closet. Was someone behind her? Was she hearing her own footsteps? While holding her breath, she lunged at the door, and with trembling hands entered the code twice before she got it right.

After the door closed, she leaned her head against the wall and slid down its slick surface. She coiled into a ball on the floor. She might be there an hour or a day; she had no way of knowing. Overloaded senses shut down. Her world went black.

.~.

She awoke with a start, ready to fight. Her heart raced as she looked around at her surroundings. Cleaning supplies and folded smocks rested on the shelves. The memory of her fight returned.

She rose, put an ear to the door, and listened… to the muffled laughter of the Superiors as they dropped off a package. Adrenaline and relief spilled through her veins. A shaky smile crossed her face as she kept her ear to the door. The vestibule doors hummed open. She counted to three and poked her head from the door.

All clear.

Fran tiptoed across the hall and the moist, warm, healing balm touched her skin. She breathed in the sweet air as the blades rotated in a blurry circle, offering her the breath of life. The motor ceased, and silence filled the vestibule.

She ran.

Jumped.

Gripped and pulled.

Bellied under the fan.

The light from beyond beckoned, and she crawled toward freedom, every tortured moment, her heart wrenched and turned in her chest.

Pete. Sweet, brave, goofball Pete. He'd believed in her. He'd loved her. He'd given her a gift that no one else ever had, yet she'd discarded it like a cheap toy. On a sob, she remembered the day he'd breathed life into her tired soul and the way he had whispered her name.

Not Wolf.

Not Fran.

But Sarah, her real name.

She hardly felt like a princess, yet mercy poured into the venting as if welcoming royalty. She thought about Ted. Would she see him again one day in the distant future, or would he be swallowed up as well? Although she'd managed to disarm her personal Beast, a monster still existed down there. A mere twelve floors below, this Beast still gave children nightmares and stole hope from the aging. Until the truth could be told, that paralyzing fear of death would continue to prey on them all and, for some, consume them wholly.

At last the light shone overhead and she lifted her eyes toward the blue skies. She took one last look behind her.

"You will be crushed," she whispered to the darkness and then crawled to freedom.

Chapter Thirty

Ted marched the length of his living pod. *That couldn't have been her.* His blood boiled cursing her stupidity. *What were you thinking?* He rubbed his forehead as if would help untangle the jumbled thoughts and make sense out of what he'd just witnessed.

She had no business being out on her own. *Next time*, he would not let her out of his sight. Next time his iron hand was going to come down on with that curly-haired terror.

Like a lion waiting to be fed, he patrolled the entry to Nissa's chamber. Since she manned Behemoth, Ted was sure she'd be able to clarify the parts of the show he'd missed. As he paced, the door hummed open. Nissa burst through, all smiles and giggles.

"Did you see that, Teddy-Bear?"

"Oh I saw it, alright."

"Wasn't that spectacular?! Nissa and Ted's voices collided as he growled. "What was she thinking?"

They paused to examine one another. Nissa perched her hands onto slender hips

"That was one of my best games ever. You *are* proud of me, aren't you?"

Ted shook his head. "My sister almost died."

"Was that *Wickerbug*? I thought it looked like her. But then again, all of the Rebels started to blur into one, so I wasn't sure." Nissa shrugged. "I will totally need to thank her when we see her next."

"Holy indifference, Nissa! You don't understand, do you?" Ted slapped the hallway table. "It wasn't just a game. The deaths weren't simply avatars. They were real people."

Nissa waved a slim hand and began to saunter away. "Oh I know. But they were Rebels, anyway—"

She recoiled as if being hit by her own words.

"I mean, except for Frannie. I would definitely have felt bad if our little Wickbug died."

She turned back to Ted wearing her best pouty-face. Ted's nostrils flared as he pulled in a controlled breath. He allowed the oxygen to take up residence in his lungs while examining her sappy expression.

"What? She didn't die, did she?" Nissa drummed her nails onto the table.

He waited until his lungs cried, "*Uncle,*" before allowing the breath to whoosh forth. "No, she didn't *die,*" he growled. "I mean I don't *think* she did. After the lights went out, she was simply gone."

Nissa placed her hands onto Ted's shoulders. "Oh Teddy. I hope she's not dead."

That word. Ted felt the ripple move from his gut to his spine and down his legs. He'd already felt the punch of that word two times in his short life. Ted looked down at this feet and shrugged away from her hold. "I hope not."

The mechanized, door greeter interrupted the conversation.

"You have a visitor."

Ted growled with frustration as he moved toward the doorway. The greeter commenced the next cycle of alert. "Ted and Nissa Monde, you have a visitor."

Ted swiped the display icon next to the door, and the face of security—the human kind, not the typical holographic version—appeared on his flat-screen.

"Can I help you?"

"Ted Monde?"

"Yes, that's me."

"I have official business of a grievous matter to discuss with you. May I come in?"

If sending a human in place of the standard holograph hadn't sent Ted's alarm clanging, this statement would have. Ted's entire body felt weak as the guard lifted his com device to auto-scan, and the greeter announced his credentials.

"Officer Gregory Reynolds. Order of the Council."

Ted held his breath, wishing for the disconnectedness of a Graphie instead of warm body. Nonetheless, he slid the door open and Officer Reynolds stepped inside.

"Ted, we have been informed that your sister, Sarah Monde, has been in violation of her house arrest status. Although we have suspicions as to why, before we make a final decree on her status, doctrine dictates we check with surviving family members as to Accountability."

"You mean you want to know where she is? Fran?" Ted laughed. "Your guess is as good as mine."

Officer Reynolds shook his head. "I'm sorry, Mr. Monde." He voice lowered. "I was afraid you'd say that."

He turned away from Ted's stare and began to fidget before clearing his throat and continuing his speech.

"Because of her Unaccountability, the Council has declared Sarah Monde... Deceased."

Air whooshed from Ted's lungs like he'd been hit in the gut, and he folded his arms around his midsection. The way the horrible words eased from the officer's lips, nice and easy—like ordering a hamburger at the Lunch Hut—repulsed Ted as much as the words themselves. He eased his breath through flared nostrils and tried to pull in another shaky lungful. His chest locked up on a sob.

Officer Reynolds flinched and looked down his nose as if a sudden stench filled the air. He turned on his heels and moved back toward the doorway.

"You can follow me to collect her belongings."

Ted's head snapped up and he glared at the detached officer's back. *Hey, your sister's dead. Come get her stuff.* He imagined yanking the moron by the collar and unloading a piece of his mind—Officer of the Council, or not.

He spoke through clenched teeth. "Yes, Officer Reynolds. Thank you."

Nissa's pouty murmurings followed Ted as he exited the pod only to be silenced when the door whooshed behind him. He followed the officer through the long maze of hallways, away from his upgraded West Wing residence and back to the East Side where he'd been raised. The familiarity ripped at his gut. He could almost hear the pounding of Wickworm's boots digging into the hard floor, trying to keep up with her big Bro. He swore he could still hear the echo of her laughter and jammed his hands into his pockets, as he stifled the urge to scream in protest.

When they reached Fran's accommodations, Officer Reynolds stepped aside, allowing Ted entry. He moved into her home, taking note of the scarcity of belongings. The refrigerator housed no icy drinks and the cupboards, nothing other than a few dusty plates. She had left an unmade bed and a bag of garbage. The transient atmosphere seemed to laugh a mocking reminder of his sister's Rebel behavior.

Ted moved to the edge of the bed, eased onto the hard mattress, and placed elbows onto knees, while he stared at the floor. He reached for a pillow and then pressed his face onto its softness while breathing in the essence of his sister—fast food and sweet honey.

Could this intangible aroma on this pillow be all that remained of the curly haired Wickworm? He breathed it in again, unable to even think of letting her go. At least Mom and Dad had lived a full life before their decline. How could it be? How could his fifteen year old sister be gone forever?

A sob ripped through his gut and seared the hollow of flesh as it shredded through his throat. He balled up the pillow and chucked it at the wall as he bellowed. The rush of blood in his head manifested as black spirals in his vision. He flopped back onto the tangle of sheets and squeezed his eyes shut as tears threatened to spill, but the lumpy bed offered no comfort.

He reflected on the plush comfort of his own West-Wing bed, and guilt raced through his veins. He hadn't taken care of his sister like had promised his mother. Sure, he'd tried to bring Frannie into his and Nissa's world. But when she resisted, he never really pushed back. Was he lazy? Selfish? Maybe both. And now? Now she was gone. Forever.

An extra hard protuberance jutted into the top his spine. Figuring Fran had left a food carton in the folds, he reached a hand behind his neck to push the object aside. Instead of crinkly aluminum, however, his hand brushed against the cool, smooth, surface of an E-reader.

A reader? He almost laughed at the audacity. The girl who couldn't even afford decent clothes somehow managed to get her hands on a reader. He dragged it around to take a look and as he turned it over in his hands, noted her initials etched into the side. Messy, like she'd used the edge of a knife, they touted her ownership. So Fran.

He gazed at it as if he'd just discovered a historic relic. It bore evidence that Fran had been a part of this room. Something tangible he could hold, unlike the invisible scent on her pillow. Ted held it to his chest and allowed himself the luxury of a few scattered memories; dancing blue eyes, ringlets like paper ribbons, and laughter so riotous it bordered on hilarity.

Finally, he sobbed for the girl he had left behind last year and the hardened teen who had replaced her when she came back. He cried for his own losses and the pain that never seemed to go away.

When he had emptied himself of memories and tears, he stood, and with Fran's old reader tucked to his side, exited her old residence.

In your unfailing love you will lead the people you have redeemed. In your strength you will guide them to your holy dwelling.

Exodus 15:13

Acknowledgements

It takes a village to write a book, and I thank all my patient and dedicated readers, friends and *awesome* family. You all share in this story.

Special thanks to you, Suni, for lifting Fran to higher highs (and lower lows).

Anita. You're a genius. The end.

M'boi's… you're the lights of my life.

Benj. My partner, friend, confidant, cheerleader and amazing man of the house. We're rocking the kingdom, Babe!

Yet, above all, *I thank Christ Jesus our Lord, who has given me strength, that he considered me trustworthy, appointing me to his service. 1 Timothy 1:12 (NIV)*

About the Author

Heather considers herself but a worker in the field with a desire to share truth through the art of a good story. In real life, she's the proud mother of two grown sons and the wife to one super-husband. In addition to the Ascension Series, Heather enjoys sharing her writing through blogs and Christian magazines, as well as traveling the U.S. on a full-time basis with her fellow Gypsy Nerd. Keep an eye out, you never know when she might roll into your hometown! If you'd like, you can follow their trail @ www.lettotravels.wordpress.com

Learn more about Heather @ www.heatherletto.com

Glossary of Terms

Agora – Similar to a modern-day mall, this highly visited hub of Impervious is well stocked with food, entertainment, and shopping.
Avatars – Video game characters operated remotely by professional gamers.
The Beast – Death or the implication of death.
Behemoth – Nissa's gaming avatar.
Canvies – Baggy, multi-pocketed trousers made of synthetic canvas-like material.
Council – The ruling party inside of Impervious.
Cybernetic vacation – A virtual-reality getaway.
Cybermoon – A cybernetic honeymoon.
D.R.A.G.O.N. – Acronym for *Drag Racing Air Generated Original Nanocycle*—a futuristic motorcycle with many cool options including JET mode.
The Decline – A disease within the city of Impervious which eats away at the mind and body of residents.
Electromagnescence – A bi-product of intense radiating energy.
East Wing (Old East, OE) – The original residential wing of Impervious. Less affluent residents dwell in the East Wing.
Feeding Trolley – A portable, mechanized, feeding device used to nourish post prime residents once unable to feed themselves. Machine components include a retractable feeding arm as well as an indwelling compartment for the food bucket storage.
Esteemed Forfeiture – An act of willingly giving up one's life in exchange for six months of fame and fortune as well as an antidote to avoid an untimely death.
Forfeiture – A resident contracted to partake in Esteemed Forfeiture.
Geiger Zombies – Fictitious, radioactive, mutant, beings leftover from the War of Annihilation.
Gen – A shortened form of, *generation,* and is used to denote a specific time period post War of Annihilation.

Graphie – A four-dimensional image (holograph) used in the city for advertising and security purposes.
Iris scan – Biometric means to ID residents in the city.
Light Genie – A flashlight which easily illuminates with the wave of a hand.
Mid-Lifer – A resident who is no longer considered a child, yet is still free from disease. This era in a resident's lifespan is typically between the ages of fifteen and twenty.
Nibbler packet – A snack.
Pod – A home much like an apartment or condo.
Post-Primer – An Impervieite who has succumbed to the decline and is no longer considered a viable resident.
The Ranch – The post prime care center similar to a nursing home.
Reader – Handheld personal computer.
Rebel – The name given to residents who are Unaccountable to the Council.
Roaming Image Transmitter (R.I.T.) - A small camera with flight capabilities controlled remotely by security. This device roams the residential hallways implementing iris scans on residents.
Surface (floor) – The top floor of Impervious rests nearest to the earth's surface and, therefore, called Surface floor.
The Seven – The highest authorities inside of Impervious made up of Marcus, his son, grandson, and four of the original creators of the city.
Superior – Members of the Council are also called Superiors because they seem impervious to the decline.
Viewing Loft – A viewing area overlooking the Agora with seating for the Council members.
West Wing – Second phase of homes built in the city. With a modern a flare and upscale technology, this section of Impervious houses the wealthier residents.

Discussion Questions

- Other than the threat of an early demise, the city of Impervious may not seem like such a horrible place to live. Imagine yourself as resident of Impervious. What type of life do you think you would live? What would be your biggest fears? Joys?

- Do you feel Fran's decision to live as an Unaccountable Rebel was born from a noble desire to await the Epoch, or do you feel her actions were triggered by life circumstances? Why?

- Have you walked through (or, maybe, even are still in the midst of) a similar time of rebellion in your own life? If so, what do you think may have been some motivating factors?

- Fran truly believed that after her loved ones succumbed to the decline, they were gone forever. Likewise, in our world, when a person passes away, we are struck with the same sense of loss. Grief can be gut-wrenchingly painful. Talk about your own experiences with loss.

- When first reading the Diary of First Gen, Fran is intrigued and hopeful, although, hesitant to rely on this account as hard fact. What discoveries help her along the way to believe in its legitimacy? What would you need to see in your own life to be given the same level of hope and assurance in the future?

- Because of what she learns from the diary, Fran chooses to test out what she had only hoped to be true. If you could speak with any figure from history about life after death, who would it be and what kinds of questions would you ask?

- It's true. Not everyone considers themselves a lover of the great outdoors! What do you think may have been the biggest struggles encountered by those who were pilgrims to the open air?

*Want to dig deeper into the allegorical nature of The Ascension Series? For a free downloadable curriculum guide visit:***http://www.heatherletto.com/#!books/cnec**

Made in the USA
San Bernardino, CA
29 August 2016